NOBLE'S
WAY

D0613560

NOBLE'S WAY

DUSTY RICHARDS

M. EVANS
Lanham • Boulder • New York • Toronto • Plymouth, UK

Published by M. Evans
An imprint of Rowman & Littlefield
4501 Forbes Boulevard, Suite 200, Lanham, Maryland 20706
www.rowman.com

10 Thornbury Road, Plymouth PL6 7PP, United Kingdom

Distributed by National Book Network

Copyright © 1992 by Dusty Richards
First paperback edition 2014

All rights reserved. No part of this book may be reproduced in any form or
by any electronic or mechanical means, including information storage and
retrieval systems, without written permission from the publisher, except
by a reviewer who may quote passages in a review.

British Library Cataloguing in Publication Information Available

Library of Congress Cataloging-in-Publication Data

The hardback edition of this book was previously cataloged by the Library of
Congress as follows:

Richards, Dusty ,
   Noble's Way / Dusty Richards
      p. cm.—(An Evans novel of the West)
   I. Title. II. Series.
   PS3568.I31523N6   1992   91-46114
   813'.54—dc20

ISBN: 978-1-59077-250-8 (pbk. : alk. paper)
ISBN: 978-1-59077-251-5 (electronic)

∞™ The paper used in this publication meets the minimum requirements of
American National Standard for Information Sciences—Permanence of
Paper for Printed Library Materials, ANSI/NISO Z39.48-1992.

Printed in the United States of America

This book is dedicated to my wife Pat, who always supported and believed in my effort, whose assistance and efforts made it possible. Linda, Charle, Judy, Velda, Jim, Becky, and Lee for his knowledge of firearms. And the dean of critiques, Dr Frank Reuter. Gracias, Amigos

Dusty Richards

Chapter One

Fat, leaden clouds skimmed the rolling sea of stirrup-tall, brown grass. Noble McCurtain held the powerful, gray horse to a walk on the dim wagon tracks. He turned in the saddle to smile reassuringly at the attractive young woman riding the bay. She gave him a nod of approval. Then she adjusted the multi-colored quilt she wore for a shawl against the cold. Luke, her seven year old son, riding on top of the pack horse, waved to him.

He acknowledged the boy before he settled back. Slowly he exhaled. How had they made it this far? Noble tried to shut the events of the past month from his mind. Something more pressing was ahead; he must find shelter. The ominous overcast meant snow, and they needed to den up or risk freezing to death from exposure. Kansas offered both Fleta Corey and himself a new start, but it also held the hazards of bitter winter weather.

Why was he so worried? Things had a way of working out for them. Even his greatest concern—fording the Arkansas River—had turned into a simple task thanks to low water.

He reined his horse beside Fleta's. "Today, we need to find and shoot a buffalo."

"But we haven't seen any," she reminded him.

"We're in buffalo country. A few always stay behind when the main herd goes south."

"What'll we do with all the meat?" The bewildered look in her blue eyes forced Noble to wonder if their escape to Kansas had been the wisest thing for them after all.

1

"Take the choicest parts. The weather's cold enough, it'll keep for days."

"What do you want Luke and me to do?" She glanced back to check on her son. He seemed so brave for his years.

"Keep a look out." He turned to the youth. "Luke! You keep your eyes peeled for a buffalo, too."

The boy smiled, pleased to be included in the plans. She had scolded Luke several times for asking Noble a lot of questions.

Noble brushed back his wind-tossed, light brown hair. He paused for a moment to admire the handsome woman beside him.

It seemed long ago that he had been forced to side with the Arkansas farm wife against the raiders who intended to use her for their own purposes.

One of the raiders had escaped, forcing Noble to periodically check their back trail, looking for the man called the Squaw Killer, Izer Goodman.

Noble squinted his eyes to check the distant rises for signs of buffalo. Somewhere, not too far ahead, he must find a place for his new family to spend the winter. Plenty of distance now separated them from Fleta Corey's outspoken neighbors and their wagging tongues. They had quickly judged her for taking him in, but failed to understand that she and the boy had no food to eat.

Three years earlier, her husband joined the Confederate Army and she'd never heard from him again. Noble was convinced Fleta's husband was an unlisted fatality. He dismissed Wilbourne Corey's existence; in Noble's book, the man measured up to a fool to leave his wife and son unattended that long if he was alive.

Noble had a personal reason for leaving Arkansas. He had spent the early war years freighting to forts in the west; the draft never caught up with him. Out of work, because of the severe cutbacks in the western military, he wandered into north Arkansas. By good fortune, he found Fleta and the boy—he had explained his case to Fleta and she understood. But there were lots of folks, both north and south, that found fault with a man who hadn't served in the military.

There were buffalo ahead. Noble spied brown spots on the horizon, like ants. He checked over the entourage, Fleta astride the bay mare, Luke perched on the packs, and two span of oxen for their future farm. At their evening meal, they would feast on a back strip from a buffalo's loin.

Fleta followed his finger, barely able to detect them. All day, she had silently fought twinges of regret. Since they'd left Arkansas, the thought that Wilbourne might still be alive nagged her. No. She'd received no word in all those years. She and Luke would have starved except for Noble McCurtain... She had made her choice. They were one—she and Noble McCurtain—she belonged to him.

Riding side by side with him warmed her. He would find them sanctuary. Never before had she been without a roof over her head, except on the move to Arkansas from Tennessee, the year Luke was born. A house, even a dugout like they'd passed earlier east of the Arkansas River, would suffice them until spring. Noble did not have to prove his worth to her. After Wilbourne, his tenderness surprised and pleased her.

Beneath her gingham dress a canvas money-belt rode on her slender hips. Over a hundred dollars in gold; the fortune meant their future. Noble insisted she carry it in case he was separated from her and Luke.

He handed her the Colt rifle. "Keep this. You and Luke move west on this road. I'm going ahead to kill the smallest buffalo I can find."

"Be careful," she said worriedly.

"I will,' he promised. His thoughts were already centered on the movement of the distant herd. He drew the heavy Hawkins .50 caliber out of the saddle boot. With all the bushwhacker's weapons, they were well armed; matched .36 Colt revolvers were in his coat pockets.

"I'll see you in a short while," Noble said to reassure her. He put heels to the ready gray horse and bolted away.

As cool air rushed by his face, Noble practiced guiding the horse with his knees. How long had it been since he'd last shot one of these shaggy beasts? Two years before, when he was freighting to the army posts.

Half mile short of the small band, he counted six buffalo. Undisturbed, they shuffled along, grazing as they went. He advanced at a cautious walk, anxious to select the youngest and most tender herd member. A yearling heifer, waxed fat on the Bluestem grass ranged behind the older cows. Noble selected her.

A dust-coated old bull seemed to sense Noble's approach. He pawed in defiance, raking up dust and grass with his front hoof. His deep bellow thundered across the land. Obviously this older animal was relegated by his age and condition to this small group of cows. Noble had no intention of messing with the ill-tempered monarch.

He dropped the knotted reins on the horse's neck and then cocked the hammer back on the .50 caliber muzzle loader. His heartbeat quickened as he coaxed the gray into a trot. He would have to depend on the horse's swiftness to bring him close enough for an easy shot on the run.

The herd caught his scent. Noble regretted the realization as they began to run, leaning forward to urge the gray to go faster.

The herd angled downhill so their junction would be in the bottom of the great depression. Horse and rider were one, racing to cut off the desperate yearling's flight. Grass tops whipped at his boots in the stirrups. The heart and muscle of the gray surged forward, drawing them closer to the heifer.

Carefully, he raised the rifle. In another hundred yards they would collide. Steady with the gait of the horse, Noble peered through the v-sights at her wooly chest behind the churning front legs. The rifle blasted. The cloud of acrid smoke smarted his eyes. He watched her crumble face first into a somersault. Tonight, they would eat tenderloin for their supper.

Noble reined up the hard-breathing gray. "Easy big man," he coaxed the great horse.

The rest of the bison were crossing the horizon, the drum of their hooves fading. Carefully he circled the downed animal on horseback. Wounded buffalo deserved lots of attention. Many times a stricken animal recovered and rose to gore an unsuspecting man on foot. Even when Noble eased down, he was prepared to quickly remount.

His hunting knife drawn, he stepped near her head. Her pig-like eyes glazed from death's throes. Noble swiftly cut her jugular and released a fountain of blood.

Grateful for his success, he checked the rise to the east for Fleta

4

and Luke. The sight of them settled him. But as he remounted, movement on the west stopped his heart.

There was no mistaking them. The spotted ponies and the feathers fluttering. A party of Indians was watching him.

Noble set the gray into a run. Headed for Fleta, he silently cursed his lack of awareness. This was Indian country; he hadn't even given them a thought. He pushed his horse harder. Filled with ideas for their defense; any moment Noble expected to hear war cries behind him.

Damn.

Chapter Two

Noble shifted in the saddle and removed one of the Colts from his coat pocket. He jammed the revolver in his waistband, not varying his hard stare from the single Indian riding toward him.

"Stay here," he told Fleta without turning around. He took out the other Colt and lay it before him on his lap. He didn't need trouble with a bunch of warriors, not while he had a small boy and a woman to look after.

The buck raised his bare, copper arm from beneath the army blanket that hung over his shoulders. What tribe did he belong to? Noble wondered and tried to remember sign language. He'd seen plenty of men use it before, but he'd not had a chance to practice it like the other freighters. Communicating with Indians never interested him before.

Noble pursed his lips. Well, Indian, one wrong move and you'll be seven feet under this grass.

He booted the gray out to close the distance between him and to keep more room between the brave and Fleta. Steadying the pistol in his lap, he reined up thirty feet short of the man who had halted his paint horse.

"Me Spotted Horse," the Indian said.

"Noble McCurtain," he answered, inspecting the brave, who wore eagle feathers in his braids.

"Make big trade," Spotted Horse indicated himself with his thumb. "Give you good furs for part of buffalo."

Noble frowned. "I don't need your furs."

"Good furs, make warm coat," Spotted Horse said, looking very somber.

Noble checked his gray who was prancing impatiently. He sighed inwardly, knowing they could never use all the buffalo meat. A lot would surely go to waste.

"You want half?" Noble asked.

Spotted Horse nodded. His horse gave a snort that seemed to reinforce his rider's approval of the trade.

"What tribe are you from?" Noble asked. There were women with the other braves which eased his concern. Indians were less likely to use treachery when they had squaws with them.

"Osage. We are plenty peaceful. No time for war."

Noble considered their situation. They looked peaceful enough, with their women and the small children. According to would-be Indian experts he had known warparties never took their families along.

"Bring me a horse and a pack of furs," Noble said, feeling the Indian would be disappointed if he didn't bargain.

"You plenty tough trader." Spotted Horse agreed with a head nod. "Osage poor. No gunpowder for guns."

That made sense. No gunpowder, no hunting. Lord, he was beginning to think like the Indian talked.

"No stealing from my camp or bothering my woman and boy," Noble warned, waving the pistol from his lap.

"Plenty good. McCurtain and Spotted Horse be good friends, yes?"

With a wry set to his mouth, Noble nodded. If the Osage were without gunpowder, what could they do? As long as they didn't steal him blind, they could share the heifer with them. But he knew Indians had little compunction about taking someone else's goods. They enjoyed a *what's yours is mine* philosophy.

Noble put the pistol back in his waistband. He signaled for Fleta to come forward.

Spotted Horse smiled broadly. "Bring you horse and furs."

"Good," Noble said, still wary of the deal.

Spotted Horse gave a wave to his companions and a loud cheer went up. They left horses, travois and even the small children on the rise. On foot, they raced for the downed animal.

Noble surmised they must be very hungry, because the men were with the women and traditionally the squaws did the butchering. But surely they didn't intend to eat the buffalo raw? Spotted Horse gave him a nod and booted his pony to join the three women and two men.

"Are they peaceful?" Fleta asked, keeping a suspicious eye on the band surrounding the shaggy, brown carcass.

"They seem to be. They're Osage. I traded half the buffalo for a horse and furs." Noble frowned as he studied them, realizing they were already eating the animal's organs. "They're starving."

"Can we trust them?" she asked.

"I think so," Noble said exchanging a nod with Luke and answered the wide eyed youth's unasked questions. "Yes, they're real Indians."

"What should we do?" Fleta asked.

"Just stay up here. I'm going down and learn all I can."

"Noble," she said worriedly, "be careful."

"I will. I'll be back to unload. You wait here." Noble rode down the slope to the butchering site.

Two men were with Spotted Horse. One short buck in his early twenties was named Rivers. The other one, Barge Oar, Noble guessed close to thirty. Barge's wife, Otter, had a bad leg.

Spotted Horse had two wives. His youngest, Mary Joseph, was a teenager with a baby. The older woman, dressed in tailored buckskin, was named Mannah. Noble guessed her age as in the late twenties. It was apparent from her striking looks that she was not an Osage, but Noble could not define her tribal origin.

The squaws had the hide peeled off the top side. Noble stepped nearby and took a strip of the loin off the back. With a nod to the women, he started back for Fleta and the boy, leading the gray. This was enough meat for them for the night. He would get more later. Cold as the air was, the carcass would not spoil.

Fleta had built a fire. She took the meat and laid it on her cutting board. Noble did not miss her apprehensive glances toward the Osage. He was glad she had not spoken her thoughts.

As he unpacked his horse, he noticed the Osage had begun a camp not far from Fleta's fire. Mary Joseph sat on the ground, nursing her baby at her swollen immature breasts. The men took up positions on the ground while the other women began cooking.

Noble saw Luke watching everything the Osage did, then returning to ask his mother questions. Noble smiled when he overheard the one about feeding the baby.

Fleta looked up from her cooking. She studied Noble's back as he stacked the pack goods and the saddles. Satisfied that he had the Indians in hand, she still couldn't feel at ease. Fleta felt confused and at the same time awed. They acted so backward. Their dress was a mixture of Indian and white man's clothing.

Finished unpacking, Noble smiled down on her. "That meat will be good."

"Yes, it will be. Thank you."

He walked to the Indian's camp, where he squatted down with the men. If necessary, he knew the Colt in his belt would be all he needed.

"Where is your home?" Spotted Horse asked.

"I'm looking for a new one."

"West," the Osage pointed. "There is a good place for a white man to winter. You shoot buffalo. Osage do much work. Plenty to eat for everyone."

"What kind of place?" Noble asked studying their dour faces.

"Big house. Good for white man."

"Who does it belong to?"

"Long gone. No one comes there."

Nobel found himself intrigued by the notion. An abandoned place might serve them as a winter headquarters. It probably was a house or structure an Indian wouldn't use.

"You smoke pipe. We make big deal," Spotted Horse said. He produced a clay pipe and packed it with brown material from a buckskin pouch.

One of the woman brought a smoking stick to light the bowl. Spotted Horse drew hard on the mouth piece, then let a small stream of smoke out of his lips. He handed it stem first to Noble. The strong smoke scorched Noble's throat and he stifled a cough as he handed the pipe back. Spotted Horse gave the pipe to Barge who drew deeply before handing it to Rivers.

"Tomorrow. We will show you the fort," Spotted Horse promised.

Fort? What did the Osage mean? Reluctant to take another puff of their pipe, yet not wanting to insult them, Noble accepted the totem with a bland face.

When he returned to eat his supper, Fleta quizzed him about the peace pipe.

"Some kind of rotten weeds," he said under his breath. "They really like it. Kept passing it around." He glanced at the setting sun before he cut up the thick browned slabs of meat. They were a day further away from Arkansas and Izer Goodman. Thank goodness.

"Luke's terribly interested in the Osage." Fleta cast a look at the boy, poised at the edge of the panniers watching the Indians.

"He'll be all right. The Indians say there is place west of here for us to winter in...a fort with a house."

"Is the house habitable?"

Noble smiled at her and shook his head. "You know as much as I do. They want to winter near us. They'll do the work for some of the game I shoot."

Fleta grimaced. "Work? The women will do it. Besides I'm not sure I want to live by Indians. You know about them because you've been all over the west. But I've never seen any like these with feathers in their hair and beads."

"That's their way. Don't worry."

Fleta didn't look up from her food. Noble knew she did not agree with his plan.

"Let's look before we pass our judgment. I'm anxious to find a place to stay. It's late December and any day winter could close in on us."

Fleta blinked at something causing Noble to twist quickly around, nearly spilling his dish. He saw the woman leading the horse toward them.

"What is she doing?" Fleta asked, puzzled by Mannah's approach. When she looked back, Noble seemed occupied with his plate again.

"What is she bringing us?"

"Your furs for half the buffalo." He smiled in amusement.

"Oh." If Noble had planned to have Indians around all winter, she would have to get used to their strange customs. She shuddered recalling their consumption of the raw liver.

Noble graciously accepted the horse's lead rope. The skins in the packs probably represented a good portion of the Osage's wealth. So far the Osage were true to their promises.

Dawn came. The light snow Noble had expected for a week frosted the tall grass. Weary and stiff from sitting up under a blanket, he'd only caught brief snatches of sleep to be on guard. Gratefully, he accepted Fleta's tea and oats. The sharp tea helped to revive him.

Spotted Horse came and squatted on the other side of the fire. "We need to go fast. Wind turns, there will be much snow. We need to camp at this place."

Noble did not question the Indian's weather forecast. He hoped this new place would not be too tumbledown to protect his family. "We'll be ready to travel soon," he promised the man.

The Osage nodded, pulled his blanket tighter, and went back to his own camp.

Fleta felt the larger flakes melt on her cheeks as she rode. The world seemed to have closed in. She could barely see the Osage women walking beside their travois laden horses. Twisting occasionally she watched her excited son on the pack horse. He was testing the snow in his open palm. His eyes were alive with excitement that escaped her. The Indians obviously fascinated Luke.

Ahead, she could see Noble, his coat speckled with snow, and his hair mussed by the wind. The sight of him was the most comforting part of this move. She was confident Noble would find a place for them before the snow turned to blistering cold.

Fleta mentally calculated the date. It was December 24, 1864, Christmas Eve. She sighed as she glanced down at the swells of the saddle. When she was little girl in Tennessee, the house was always warm and filled with the smell of popcorn and molasses candy on this day. There were always toys to open Christmas morning, usually small animals her father had whittled from wood.

Then Wilbourne Corey had come into her life. The tall quiet man, six years her senior had come to court her. Wilbourne had not been a rake or braggart. Fleta's mother had often reminded her that Wilbourne was serious—a man of substance—he worked hard, and was not inclined to drink heavy or gamble. A pillar of a man, not a man to abandon her. Fleta felt a pang of conscience as she rode. Had she been the one to abandon Wilbourne?

But her mother had not known of war and how it would drag a man away from his wife and son. Wilbourne had ignored her pleas and gone off for a bloody senseless war and left the two of them... Fleta shivered under her coat. They might have starved if Noble had not come along. Since she'd had no word in three years, surely Wilbourne Corey had died for his cause.

"Fleta?" Noble asked, his gray horse huffing great clouds of steam beside her. "Are you all right? You worry me." He looked intently into her eyes.

"I'm fine, this snow is upsetting me," she said with a brittle smile. She watched Noble lift Luke from the pack horse.

"Spotted Horse says we're close to wherever they're taking us. But we need to make camp 'til the snow lets up."

"But," she began, her throat knotted with conflicting emotions as she stood beside the horse; her legs weak from poor circulation. "It's Christmas Eve, Noble."

He blinked and pushed back his hair. "Is it?"

"Yes and I don't have a thing for anyone," Fleta lamented. How could she make the holiday up to Luke? She practically fell in Noble's arms. He held her tight to comfort her.

"I'll make it up to you soon, Fleta. I promise," he said softly, concealing his frustration.

She sniffed and tried to regain her composure. "I'm sorry, Noble. It's the damned snow. Where's Luke?"

"He's right here," he gestured at his side.

She leaned her forehead on Noble's shoulder. Tears and melted snowflakes mingled on her face. It was the snow that had depressed her so.

Christmas day arrived under a blanket of low and threatening gray clouds. Fleta rose in a flurry of snow flakes that had fallen on the blankets she and Luke shared. Noble was studying something on the horizon, his breath escaping in steamy vapors. Then Fleta saw it, and hurried to stand with him. A small fort on a rise, less than a quarter mile away.

"Is that the place?" she asked through chattering teeth.

"Yes." He hugged her to his side. "Spotted Horse said it was empty."

"Who owns it?"

"We do."

"But what if the army or the owners come back?"

"I guess we'll move out." Noble twisted her around and put his cold hands to her cheeks and lowered his mouth to hers. His hard eager lips, hungry with desire, warmed her.

She smiled. "We'll call it McCurtain's Fort."

"All right," Noble agreed, pleased with her name for the place. "Come on, we need to see the home the good Lord and the Osages have provided for us."

"Merry Christmas, Noble McCurtain," Fleta said with a sad smile.

"Merry Christmas, Fleta McCurtain," he said before hurrying off to get the horses and stock.

She stood alone. In that moment, in the middle of snowy Kansas, she felt that they were married in the eyes of God. Her son and the Osages were the witnesses. Yes, she decided, from now on she would be Fleta McCurtain and never again regret leaving Arkansas.

As soon as he swung off his horse in the gateway, Noble began sizing up the fort. Inside the hewed log post wall was a courtyard close to a hundred by hundred-fifty feet. A post or store was in the center. The leather hinges on the front door were rotten. He forced it open and entered. Although dusty and cobwebbed, the low ceiling caused him to smile. It would be a cosy place to winter.

"Come on in to your house," he shouted to Fleta, and stood aside to allow her entrance.

Noble left her examining the house. He went to inspect the fort. There were stable sheds built off the side walls. Followed by the silent Spotted Horse, he stopped to examine the stone walled well. He dropped a packed snowball in it and was rewarded a few moments later by the reassuring splash of water.

Noble walked back to the gateway and looked to the south. The plank gates were down and he decided they would require much repair to rehang. But when he viewed the white sea beyond, he was pleased with their new home.

"Spotted Horse, who does this fort belong to?"

"You and me." The Indian pointed at Noble then himself.

"No." Noble tried to explain. "Is this an army fort?"

"No, long ago trader was here.

That solved the mystery for Noble. Some trading company had apparently built this as an outpost, then abandoned it.

"It's a good place," he said, smiling with gratitude at the Indian.

"Plenty good."

"Noble!" Luke came running. "We even have rats in the new house."

"What's a house without rats?" Noble laughed and Spotted Horse joined in.

As he approached the house, he wondered how his new wife was accepting all this. With surprise, he watched the two Osage men carrying Fleta's things in the front door.

"Wait!" he shouted. "I'll do that."

"No," Spotted Horse said, restraining Noble with his hand. "We help."

For a moment Noble questioned their motive. This was women's work—at least in the Indians eyes—so they must be paying Fleta and himself a high compliment by humbling themselves with such activity. Damn, he had a lot to learn about Indians.

In the fireplace Fleta built a small fire which produced not only warmth, but seemed to drive away a cold lingering spirit that inhabited the small house. She surveyed the room with satisfaction. A worn broom applied to the hard packed floor would make the place look even better. She had a roof and a home. Noble had even repaired the front door, so now it seemed like a secure haven.

Later Mannah brought her some cold, cooked meat to heat up. Fleta found herself liking the tall, handsome woman, who dressed in buckskins decorated with beads and quills. She wondered why

Mannah was childless, perhaps even barren. Her beauty and movements were graceful as a swan. Fleta initially was irritated by the Indian woman's habit of giggling, but she had begun to dismiss it as a childish habit they never outgrew. Fleta felt a bond growing between herself and Mannah.

Fleta found a good supply of dry buffalo chips in a lean-to behind of her kitchen. There was even a small amount of wood she must ration.

Luke was in and out of the house reporting on the tepee raising going on outside. Breathlessly, he told his mother how the travois poles became the main support for the tepees. And he further explained in a voice filled with awe, of the paintings on the side of the tepees, drawings of horses, buffalo and hand prints.

After fixing the door, Noble fetched water for tea, then left to check on the livestock. Mary Joseph and her baby came to sit beside her fireplace. Fleta felt a twinge of jealousy as she watched the young mother nurse the child. Noble needed a son of his own.

Noble viewed the horses pawing the snow for grass. The four patient oxen were waiting to graze behind them.

"We will watch them," Spotted Horse assured him. "At night we will bring them inside the fort grounds. There are many thieves, besides the buffalo wolves."

"Thanks," Noble said, his mind occupied with laying plans. Tomorrow we'll go kill another buffalo before the winter catches us."

"Yes," the Osage agreed with a wide grin. "This is a god damn good place."

"Yes it is," Noble smiled at the profanity. He recalled an Indian who lived around a western post. The men called the Indian Son-of-a-Bitch. He used the word for everything, hello— goodbye— every other word that came out of his mouth was the curse.

He smiled ruefully. "Spotted Horse? Do you have a fine fur to trade me? A mink?"

The Osage shifted the army blanket over his shoulder. "Mink?"

"A nice soft fur."

The Indian nodded. Noble dug out a pocket knife for the trade.

Spotted Horse shook his head. "No. Fur be a gift for you."

"No. We trade," Noble insisted.

The Osage left Noble standing in the snow at the fort's gate. He returned in a few minutes with an impressive looking scarf of white fur. For a moment, Noble wondered which of the Osage's wives had lost such a mantle. He swept the pelt onto his shoulder and slapped the folding knife in Spotted Horse's hand.

"Trade," Noble said firmly.

Spotted Horse nodded. With that settled, Noble trudged to the house. He passed the others busy raising the second tepee and grinned at Luke watching them. Wide eyed, the youth investigated every movement the Indians made, but he remained respectfully back and out of their way.

Noble pushed open the door to their new home then closed it with his hip.

"Here," he said, looping the fur around Fleta's neck.

She gasped at the feel of the soft skin around her neck. "What are you doing?"

Noble pulled her tightly against him. "It's a surprise."

"Oh, Noble, you shouldn't have. It feels beautiful." She looked up at him with a smile.

"Merry Christmas, Mrs. McCurtain," he said, squeezing her against his lean body. He enjoyed the proprietary sound of the "Mrs."

"Let's have some tea." She lightly kissed his lips.

They were finishing their tea and savoring the privacy of their moment together, when Luke burst in the front door. "Noble! Spotted Horse said to come with your gun right now! We got plenty trouble coming!"

"What is it, Luke?" Noble removed the Colt from his right coat pocket and followed the youth out the door.

"Three riders dressed in bear skins. Spotted Horse says they're bad men."

"Who are they?" Fleta asked, following them outside.

"Damned if I know. Luke, you stay here with your mother. Fleta get the other guns ready just in case."

"But..."

"No buts. Unless they have a deed to this place they can go to hell for all I care." Noble turned with the .36 Colt in his right hand and went to join the Indians gathered at the gate.

Spotted Horse apparently knew the strangers since he had told Luke that they were bad. Who were they? No telling, but whoever they were, Noble was ready for trouble. The heavy revolver in hand reassured him as he headed for the gate.

Chapter Three

Under a glaring patch of cold sun, Noble watched the three bearded riders come abreast. Splashing snow, their horses breathed heavily. Saddle leather creaked. When the man in the middle pushed up his hat brim, Noble felt a sharp stab of fear. It was Izer Goodman.

An older man on Izer's right cradled a rifle in a fringed sheath; he broke the silence first. "All you blanket-ass Injuns get the hell out of our fort."

"Damn my sore eyes," Izer said with mocking sarcasm, "why, it's my old pal Noble McCurtain." There was nothing friendly in his tone.

Noble stood his ground, arms crossed, the pistol in his hand.

"You know him?" the man on Izer's right asked.

"Sure do. He's done got him an Osage squaw to love, boys!" Izer's cutting laughter caused Noble's jaw to clench. The bushwhackers had called Izer the squaw killer.

"What's your business here?" Noble demanded with more confidence than he felt.

"You claiming this place?" Izer asked, resting an elbow on his saddle horn.

"Me and this pistol are," Noble answered without finching.

"He's tough talking, Izer," the older man mocked. His laughter was interrupted by a hacking cough. In disgust he spit out a yellow wad of phlegm.

"This old man's Red Barber." Then Izer gestured to the younger man on his left. "And Tennessee Dawson. Boys, meet Noble McCurtain."

Noble did not acknowledge the introductions.

Izer scrubbed his whisker-stubbled mouth with his hand as if considering another tactic.

"Boy," he directed his speech to Noble, "we've run all these black asses off before. But you can stay and be a part of us—or else."

"Else what?" Noble shot back.

"You don't aim to die over some flea-bitten redskins and a damned old fort, do you?" Izer demanded in disbelief.

"Somebody may die, but more'n likely it will be you all."

"Tough bastard," Tennessee growled as if itching to do something.

"Yeah," Izer said. "Reckon we'll just have to kill him, then we can have that Osage squaw of his. She must be something to behold."

"Izer, take your friends and leave," Noble warned. A fury boiled over inside him.

"Boy!" Izer said, his dark eyes narrowing. "I intend to feed you to the magpies and rape every Osage squaw in there."

"Yeah!" Red shouted, preparing to charge his horse.

A rifle shot out. The three men bolted upright, checking their horses. Before they had full control of their mounts, Noble had the Colt cocked and ready. For a moment he wondered who had fired the shot, but he kept his attention firmly fixed on the three men in front of him.

"Who the hell is she?" Izer demanded, fighting with his horse and peering over his shoulder at someone behind Noble.

Ready for any move they made, Noble's lips twitched briefly as he realized that Fleta had fired the shot. He remembered how she had helped him the day they battled the bushwhackers. Izer never stayed for any of that fight, for like a coward he'd left at the first sign of resistance.

"That's my wife," Noble said. He watched Mannah come forward and give Spotted Horse the Colt rifle. The tide of the encounter just changed; Noble waited for their next move.

Izer's face was black with rage. "You ain't seen the last of us, Noble McCurtain. Next time we ain't coming in here peaceful. That goes for the gawd damn Osages too."

"Come again, Izer and we'll nail your hides to our wall."

Izer looked as though he might try something, but instead he jerked his horse about savagely. "Come on, boys. Let' s get the hell out of here!"

Noble noticed the leering expressions as the man looked past him at his wife. His finger tightened on the trigger. His lecherous contemptible stare raised Noble's fury. Then Izer turned and led his men away. It was the not the first time Izer had run away from a fight with Noble.

"I'm sorry, Noble," Fleta apologized as she reached him. "I know you could have handled it."

Noble did not answer her. His attention was still riveted on the three men as they became smaller and the distance between them widened across the snow covered landscape. Finally, Noble sighed. Those bastards would be back. "Don't fret none. You did the right thing sending Spotted Horse the rifle. It helped get rid of that scum."

"They don't talk so big against two guns," Spotted Horse said, sounding smug.

"They're bullies," Noble said. He turned to the Osage. "You keep the rifle. We need to be ready for that bunch. I've got a hunch they'll be back."

The Osage grunted. "I told you there are worst things than buffalo wolves."

"Right," Noble agreed, walking back to the house with Fleta. He wished the three men had not seen her. There was no telling when they would be back or what would happen when they did return.

Fleta walked beside him, carrying the Hawkins rifle. "Who else will come?"

"In the spring, I figure settlers will start appearing around here," he said, anxious to turn her fears away from Goodman's bunch.

"Settlers?" she quizzed, wondering what he meant.

"Sure, they'll be a lot of folks looking for new land. They'll need things, too—supplies. We got us a good place for a store," Noble said. He was deeply engrossed in his plans as they entered the house.

"Who has the money to buy such things?" Fleta asked skeptically.

"Yankees do. They'll be itching for supplies by the time they get here. Fleta, those northern states are rich, not like Arkansas."

She shook her head. "Why did those bushwhackers come to rob us?"

"Fair game. No law, no one to stop them or protect people."

"Noble," she began firmly. "Next time those three men come back, I'll lower my sights so I won't waste the shot in the sky."

He squeezed her shoulder. "I'll reload your rifle. Woman, a grizzly bear couldn't get past you."

A frown furrowed her brows. "Are bears out there, too?"

"No."

Fleta was not fully reassured by his tone. She watched him reload the Hawkins. "You're sure there are no grizzlies out there?"

He looked up and shook his head. "Never seen one in Kansas. Ask Spotted Horse, if you don't believe me."

"Well, I believe you," she said, still envisioning twelve-foot-tall bears.

"Izer Goodman is a far worse enemy," Noble said, setting the muzzle loader by the door.

"Can you tell me if anything else is going to happen today?" she asked.

"Yes." He swept her up in his arms. "Tonight, I'm going to love you."

She struggled half-heartedly to escape. "Well, go get some water then. I'm filthy and you have whiskers like a grizzly." She wrinkled her nose at him.

He released her and rubbed his face. His beard stubble wasn't quite as bad as a bear's, but bad enough.

"I kinda smell like a horse, too," Noble admitted, and winked at her. "After I get your water, I need to take Spotted Horse some more ammunition."

"More ammunition?"

"Yes, they need to help us guard this place."

"But what if—"

"Fleta," Noble interrupted patiently, "the Osages are defenseless without ammunition. They need us right now and we need them."

She frowned and murmured, "I suppose so."

Noble drew several buckets of water so his family could take a bath. He smiled at Luke's reluctance, but saw the determined look in Fleta's eye and knew the lad could not escape. Satisfied they had enough water, Noble took two dozen brass cartridges to Spotted Horse's tepee.

Mannah drew the flap aside and showed him into the smoky interior. The small fire's light shown on the Osage's face. Noble took a seat beside the man, dreading another round of smoking the peace pipe.

"I brought you some shells for that rifle," Noble said, handing over the rounds. "You and Rivers and Barge must help me guard our place with that gun. It isn't a buffalo gun, but it would stop the likes of those outlaws today."

Spotted Horse reached for the carbine and set it across his lap. "Plenty gawd damn good. No one will come here but friends. The Osage will guard this fort."

"We need to go hunting tomorrow."

The Indian shook his head. "There will be more snow. Sleep and rest, then we go."

Perhaps he knew more about the weather than Noble did. He thanked the Indian and excused himself. Outside, he studied the star-studded sky and questioned the Indian's forecast. Shaking his head, he went back into the small house.

Fleta was washing her leg by the fire light. She instinctively drew her skirt down at his appearance.

"What did Spotted Horse say?" she asked.

"The Osage will protect us. They will keep their word." He paused. "There sure ain't many Osage left."

She resumed her bathing. Why had he not stayed just a a little longer, so she could have finished. She studied him for a moment before proceeding with her bath. Noble did not seem to be paying any attention to her. He was looking at something on the wall.

"Why don't the Osage have more children?" she asked curiously.

He shrugged. "Diseases, I guess. Indians been dying of white man's diseases for a long time."

"I guess you're right. Oh, you can start your bath now."

A grin tilted his lips. "Are you hinting I smell like an Osage?"

"Well..."

Noble pulled his shirt away and lowered his nose to it. He grimaced. "Guess I do at that."

They both laughed, then he followed her sharp look up at the sleeping boy in the loft and guiltily they became quieter.

Fleta busied herself picking up clothing while he bathed. Tonight, they would commence their private life again. A small tinge of excitement coursed through her. The days on the trail had been long, tiring and suspenseful. Their affection had been limited to a hug or a quick kiss, but they were home at last.

She took pains to carefully shave Noble's chapped face, feeling a certain pleasure looking into his eyes. After she finished, she prepared their blankets on the floor.

When Noble joined her, they rekindled their long suppressed passion. Afterwards, they lay exhausted in each other's arms.

Noble held Fleta securely by his side. Before his heavy lids fell shut, he remembered one last vision—the leering face of Izer Goodman, the squaw killer.

The following morning, to Noble's dismay, Spotted Horse's forecast for more snow was accurate. He worried about their dwindling food supply, but the continuing snowfall and the cold spell that followed kept Noble close to the fort for five days.

When the weather finally cleared and began to warm, Noble went to see Spotted Horse. "One man must go with me hunting. Two must stay and guard the fort."

"Rivers can go. He is good man. Barge and I will protect this place," Spotted Horse said.

"Good, tell him we leave shortly." He left the Indians and went back for his rifle and the provisions that Fleta had prepared.

"Noble," she said hesitantly, "don't be gone longer than two days if you can help it."

He raised his hand and gently stroked her cheek. "As soon as we get a few buffalo, we'll be back."

She pulled his wool coat together. "I know, I just worry about you."

Rivers joined Noble in the yard. The Indian was a short, powerful man, his face flatter and his eyes more almond shaped than the other Osages. He wore a turban around his head and a stiff buffalo coat hung to the tops of his high top boots.

Noble sensed that the man spoke some English when he felt like it. As they mounted up, Noble wondered if Rivers would talk to him.

Sun warmed the snow-blanketed prairie. The glare caused Noble to squint. But his companion used a narrow wood mask—notched for his nose—to cut down the snow's blinding whiteness.

"Small herd," Rivers said, pointing to some distant dots.

"Let's go slow. I've seen men shoot them at a distance and not have to charge in." Noble dismounted, anxious to stretch the muscles in his legs. If they cold maneuver close enough to drop one of the buffalo and not scare the others away, his chances of killing a second one would be better. By this method, they could down several buffalo before the animals discovered they were being shot at.

Working downwind and leading their mounts, they positioned themselves as close as Noble dared. Rivers held the gray's reins while Noble laid the hexagon barrel across the seat of his saddle. His first shot crumpled a large bull. Both men grinned at each other, the herd never seemed to notice. Noble hastily reloaded. Carefully measuring the distance he took a bead on the closest animal, a young bull. The herd, oblivious to the first downed buffalo, continued to paw the snow for their grazing. The rifle cracked, but this time Noble's target bawled in pain. Either he had shot too far back or the gun did not fire as well. The wounded bull staggered forward then sat down dog fashion. His protests spooked the others into a clumsy, snow-churning gallop.

"Good hunter," River said as the second buffalo toppled over in silence. "See plenty white men shoot all day never kill one buffalo."

"They were sportsmen," Noble tried to explain as he reloaded the .50 caliber rifle.

"Plenty bad shots." Rivers shook his head.

"Well," Noble said, sheathing the Hawkins in the saddle boot, "some day they'll make better cartridge guns than those guys use, then I'll buy one." He wasn't sure Rivers understood.

They rode down to cut the buffaloes' throats and bleed them. The Osage women and two of the men could come back the next day and slaughter them. There would be plenty of meat for the fort, Noble decided as he studied the scarlet snow where the steaming blood had pooled. Tonight, everyone could feast on the long purple slabs that Rivers extracted. Nothing would be wasted, even the animals' small brains would be used to tan their wooly hides.

The ride home was easy in the powdery snow. Flush from his successful hunt, Noble considered his new position in life with Fleta and the boy, plus a handful of Osages—a strange alliance. Yet, he began to feel confident they would make it through the winter.

Noble schemed as he rode. He needed all the horses he could muster to make a ride to Fort Leavenworth for those supplies to sell next spring. He would need them when the migration began. A wagon would be too cumbersome to drive back during the winter, either getting stuck in thawing ruts or bucking drifts. No, he needed a pack string. He would speak to the Osage chief about using their mounts. Funny, he wasn't sure if Spotted Horse was a chief; the Indians never mentioned it one way or the other. He just seemd to be their spokesman.

That evening, still high from the hunting expedition, he lay on his back beside Fleta. He studied the shadowy underside of the shake roof that was illuminated by the fireplace's flames.

"I'm going to Fort Leavenworth next month," he said quietly. "I'll put us in a stock of supplies, so come next spring, we'll be ready for the people moving west."

"What if the owners of this place come back?"

"They can go to hell. We've cleaned this mess up and we're going to hold on to it."

Fleta looked at the hard, obstinate set of his jaw and smiled. She laid an arm across his chest. It would be impossible to convince him that this place was not his.

The weather grew milder the following week. An entire tribe of Wichitas arrived at the fort on one of the clear warm days. They were loaded down with horses, children, dogs and travois. Noble sensed they were peaceful. They camped outside the wall, as if being near the structure was some form of security for them.

Noble found himself in an awkward position. These new arrivals expected to trade their furs, but he had nothing to barter. The Indians' pack horses were loaded down with fox, mink, bobcat and even a few beaver furs. Noble spotted wolf skins and deer hides that had been beaten into soft yellow buckskin. The lack of something to trade weighed heavily on his mind. Finally he hit upon an idea and went to discuss it with Spotted Horse at his tepee.

"You tell the Wichitas that I'll take their furs and bring them back goods from Fort Leavenworth," he explained to the Osage.

Spotted Horse shook his head. "They don't trust white man. You pay now, keep the furs."

"Hell's bells! That's my problem. If I had something, I would trade with them now," Noble said with exasperation.

"No good, they no give you furs."

"Get Chief Tall Timber to come to council. I'll take some Wichitas with me. When I sell the furs, they can get what they want in return."

"Probably have to take a squaw or two along. The women own the furs. A man would get the wrong supplies."

"Fine. I get twenty percent for trading," Noble said.

"You do what you want with the money. Wichitas never understand money things."

Noble started to protest. Perhaps the Osage didn't understand either. He would have his council with Tall Timber and their store would show a profit the first year in business.

The idea worked. Noble selected Rivers to help him with the pack horses on the journey. A Wichita sub-chief named No-Eyes, whom Noble suspected was far-sighted was assigned to accompany him along with three squaws. They were all older women and very fat. Noble wondered if they could ride as fast as he wanted to go. Spotted Horse assured him they were good as any man on horseback.

The head Osage's weather forecast had given Noble ten thawing days to make his round trip.

Noble shook his head, looking over his odd entourage when they reached Independence, Missouri on the fifth day. Curious townspeople came out to see the invaders. Giggling squaws, solemn Rivers, and No-Eyes kept the horses in line through the traffic though some of the Indian ponies were terrified by the wagons, buggies and rigs.

Patterson's Mercantile loomed before them with a great set of stairs leading to the porch. Noble considered it a reputable firm.

"Everyone stay close," he said to the Wichita chief. Noble dismounted the gray and handed the reins to Rivers, mounted the stairs then pushed open the bell-tinkling door.

A balding man removed his glasses and looked Noble up and down cautiously. "May I help you?"

"Name's Noble McCurtain, I've come to sell some furs."

"Yes sir, Cedric Patterson at your sevice." The men shook hands.

"Mister, I'll tell you right off. I need to be on my way shortly and I have three Wichita women out there you'll need to satisfy with trade goods."

"Certainly, young man. We have a reputation—"

"I know," Noble interrupted. "That's why I stopped here."

"Alex," the man called out to a clerk who was hardly older than Noble. "Mr. McCurtain, this is my son Alex. Alex, go outside and price his furs. He is in a big hurry to get home."

"Certainly, father." Alex's handshake was powerful. Noble took an instant liking to the owner's son.

Together they went out to the mudddy street. The giggling squaws had attracted a few gray-whiskered drunks out of the saloons. Uneasy already, Noble became very nervous when one of the women dismounted and squatted to urinate. He tried to hear Alex's comments about the furs and wondered how to avoid an incident. Noble's responsibility for the girl-like threesome included herding them safely home after their trading was completed.

He heard someone in the crowd shouting about the old days when they bedded some squaws. The women might be willing, Noble decided grimly, but his role as chaperon precluded any such activity on the women's part. The Wichitas would be alienated if their women did not return with him, all his future business with the Indians would be lost.

"Rivers!" Noble shouted. "You and No-Eyes take the women inside and start shopping." He feared he might already be too late to stop any trouble. "I'll be right back, Alex. Your prices sound fair, unload the furs." He pushed through the unbudging and twisting pack horses. One of the white men was kissing a squaw.

"Get away!" he shouted. "They all have syphilis!" He jerked the man away from the woman and shoved him into the crowd of leering drunks.

A few men moved back at his words, but others were talking trade in sign language with the squaws. Noble was certain they had no designs on the furs.

The blast of his Colt overhead drew a swift cessation to the negotiations. The men fell over themselves backing up. "Get in the store," he ordered the fat squaws. "Any of you men want to die, come one step closer."

No-Eyes took charge and marched the threesome, who had turned solemn, up the muddy street, onto the porch and then inside Patterson's front door.

"The marshal will be here shortly," Alex said ruefully when Noble rejoined him.

"Why?"

"He hates shooting in the city limits."

"I have no wish to be detained. What will it cost me?" Noble asked.

"Two dollars."

Noble shrugged. "Pay him and take it off my account. I need to go get some things out of the store and to keep an eye on those damned squaws."

"You did rather well out here." Alex grinned. "I'll handle the marshal."

Inside the store, Noble noticed that the goods were higher priced than he had imagined, but he realized that in wartime such rises were inevitable. He fretted that the money from Fleta's money belt might not pay for his planned order. His shoulders sagged as he watched the squaws rush about choosing things.

But when Cedric Patterson told him that the furs would tally over four thousand dollars, he was stunned. The man explained the sum was a rough total, and the end calculation would require hours. Noble considered the unbelievable profit.

Even though the Wichita women piled up mounds of goods which he doubted their horses could carry home, Noble planned not to spend any of Fleta's money. He walked around to study their purchases: brightly colored material, pot, pans, knives, axes, and beads.

After the staff added up all the squaw's purchases, Cedric showed Noble a two thousand dollar credit to the account in his name. Of course, the total could be higher when the furs were better appraised, Patterson assured him.

What had Spotted Horse said? He shook his head, still in awe and amazed at the turn of events. The Osage had told him to handle the trade in a white man's way and let the Wichitas trade for what they wanted. There was no need in explaining to the strutting squaws—by their book they had bested him. He ordered five hundred dollars in merchandise for the store, his family and the Osage. He felt confident his pack horses could carry that much back.

When Alex came inside, Noble looked up with a wry smile. "What did the law say?"

Alex tugged on his right ear in a gesture of apparent amusement. "He said to tell our customer that he would be glad to see the rear ends of his horses leaving town and not to ever shoot off your so-and-so pistol in downtown Independence."

Noble grinned. "Thanks, Alex. I'm obliged."

"No problem, Mr. McCurtain. We appreciate your business. We've unloaded your pack string. My helpers will help reload them."

He reached out and shook Alex's hand. "It's been my pleasure. I'll send for an order later this summer and you can have a freighter bring it to me."

"Mr. McCurtain, try this hat on," Cedric Patterson said, standing behind him. "I see you go bareheaded, but this is what many of the military officers are wearing now. A man in Philadelphia by the name of Stetson made it." He held out a high crowned, wide brimmed, cream-colored hat.

Noble looked at it with interest. He tried it on, but since he was unaccustomed to the feel of any kind of headgear, he deliberated buying the hat.

"It will fit better if you dampen the band," Alex suggested.

"How much does it cost?"

The store owner smiled broadly. "Consider it a gift. We appreciate your business."

Noble fitted the hat to his head, thanked both men and walked out on the porch in the afternoon sun. The hat shaded his eyes and pleased him. He noticed two stern faced deputies were standing nearby. The excited, magpie-chattering squaws were nearly through packing their things aboard the horses. River and No-Eyes obviously had the women well in hand and things seemed to be going smoothly.

The packing complete and everyone mounting up, Noble swung onto the saddle. He had plenty of stock for the store and everyone else at the fort, plus fifteen hundred dollars on the books. He could hardly wait to tell Fleta about their good fortune.

He looked over the train, then satisfied they were ready, he waved with a wide swing of his new hat to 'move out'. Gawk if you like, he silently told the nosey townspeople. I'm a rich man headed for home. He touched the brim of his new hat for two finely dressed ladies on the sidewalk. Behind him he could hear the giggle of the Wichitas, probably giving coy glances to the men they passed.

Even the prospect of the long ride home did not dampen his spirits. Spotted Horse's weather forecast was holding accurately and the clear Kansas sky held little threat.

On the return journey, they re-crossed the fresh streams and rivers. At night they camped, unloading the supplies then reloading them in the predawn to get an early start on each day. Noble rode in front of the procession. Sometimes he scouted a mile or so ahead to find a campsite or a better pass through the lowlands near a river to avoid marshy ground. He became saddle weary and calculated they would reach home in another day. He knew the horses were loaded heavy and thus did not make the same miles on the return trip.

"The Wichitas speak of you as a great friend," Rivers said, joining him. They watched the line of pack horses go off a sharp bank and splash through shallow creek.

"Good," Noble said. He would like to do more business with the tribe in the future, especially in view of the business just completed.

"Who was the angry man in the streets?" River asked.

It took Noble a moment to realize that he meant the marshal. "That was the white man's law."

"He was not happy with our horses in the street," Rivers said.

"Nor was he happy with me shooting my pistol off," Noble said with a laugh, realizing how the Osage must have fretted on this matter for days.

"I do not like Missouri," Rivers said, then he rode off to help the squaws get a stubborn horse out of the water.

Noble shook his head as he watched them pull and whip the balking horse until the pony finally gave up and came out of the stream. He didn't like Missouri either.

Later that night, he lay in his bedroll, his eyes heavy. Wolves howled nearby.

One more day and he would be back in Fleta's arms. There was so much to tell her. They were rich and he still had her gold coins, plus a great stock of store goods to sell.

Noble woke abruptly to find Rivers squatted beside him. The wolves sounded closer.

"Wolves," the Indian hissed. "Not real wolves."

Noble peered at the man through sleep-gritted eyes. In the starlight, he could make out grim features. The Osage would never wake him unless he was certain there was a threat. Noble listened to the sleepy grunts from the nearby horses, but there were no sounds from the wolves. The silence was heavy and yet loud with an undefined force.

Filled with uneasiness, Noble reached for his pistol and rose in a crouch. The cold air quickly found him and dissipated the bedroll's warmth. He tapped his face with the gun barrel, the sour powder smell drifting to his nostrils.

Something was wrong out there in the darkness. Noble tensed, waiting.

Chapter Four

In Noble's absence, Fleta became restless and apprehensive. She tried to stay busy; noting with some relief that Spotted Horse patrolled the fort with the Colt rifle resting in his thick arms.

To reassure herself, she appraised the situation. She no longer held any fear about the Osage's loyalty and felt if the fort came under attack, the Wichitas would help defend the place. Only fools would try anything against a force this size. Besides, she expected Noble back in a week—if the weather held.

To occupy her time, Fleta planned a vegetable garden for the coming season. It would contain all the things she had missed during the hard winter months. The mere thought of corn on the cob, beans, peas and greens made her mouth water. She had strung a line outside to dry clothes and, when she wasn't washing, she aired the quilts, another way of passing the long days.

That first evening, she found no sleep at all. Tossing and turning without Nobles's strong arms and warmth, she finally got up and sat huddled under a blanket. Fleta envisioned a hundred possible disasters that might befall her man. She finally steeled herself. He simply was going to get supplies and would be back safely.

In the morning, the sun became a bright globe, thawing the earth under Fleta's small feet encased in the fur-lined boots Mannah made for her.

Mary Joseph and the baby were always nearby. Even Otter, who kept to herself all the time, finally came to see the strange woman who sunned her blankets. Fleta was amused at their bewildered looks. Perhaps the Indians thought she was performing some strong medicine ritual.

She learned that Mannah was not an Osage, but Fleta could not pronounce the name of her tribe. Spotted Horse's older wife seemed happy enough with him, and she acted motherly toward the younger wife, Mary Joseph. Since she was childless, she must have resigned herself to the presence of a second wife. Fleta was not certain she would be so tolerant.

Fleta surmised Indian girls married at a very young age. One swollen-bellied Wichita girl was hardly more than twelve years old. But Fleta shrugged philosophically. Who was she to judge? Perhaps she was jealous, wanting to bear Noble a son. She took out her frustrations on the blankets, flailing them wildly.

The Indian women giggled and Fleta asked Mannah why they were so amused.

"They want to know if you are chasing the evil spirits away with your beating?"

"Tell them yes," Fleta confided with a smile. Almost immediately, she regretted teasing Mannah, but she could not admit she was beating them simply because she was worried about Noble.

"They want to know if you are with child?"

Flet felt her cheeks flush. She shook her head sadly. "No."

A large shadow from overhead drew the women's attention. Fleta squinted to see the giant eagle pass over them. His snow-white head glistened; he glided, on a broad wing span, with little effort. She watched until he was gone beyond the top of the fort's wall.

"Ma, that was an eagle," Luke pointed out as he joined her.

"Yes, I saw him."

"The Indians think eagles are magic."

"Maybe they are, Luke," she said, tousling his fair hair. "Where have you been?"

"Oh, at the Wichita camp. They have some new puppies."

"That's nice," Fleta said, wondering if her son had watched the delivery of the canines.

"May I have one, mamma?"

"We better wait and ask Noble."

Luke agreed and rushed off. Fleta sighed. She'd have to make sure that Luke took a bath, especially if he had been handling Indian dogs.

By the sixth day, her anxiety increased until she could hardly sit still. Fleta closed her eyes . . . she started when Spotted Horse came in the front door. His brown face wore a grim expression, enough to cause her heart to quicken.

"Someone has traded whiskey to the Wichitas. They are starting to celebrate.

"Who could have done that?" she asked, shaken by the news.

"The three men you shot at, I think," he said.

"Spotted Horse . . . what will the Wichitas do?"

The Osage shook his head. "They are friendly people. Maybe only dance."

Fleta thought for a moment, then she ordered, "Get Chief Tall Timber!"

He looked down at the floor. "No. A chief would not listen to a woman. Barge and I will guard this place."

"Send your women and the children in here."

"Thank you," he said quietly. "No one will come here and bother you." Spotted Horse nodded then hurried away.

Fleta wanted to ask him several questions, but when he was gone, she did not want to go after him. She looked up when Luke came in the back door.

"You'll have to stay in the house," she said, her tone sharper than intended.

"Why?" Luke's blank look angered her.

"Luke, this is very serious. Believe me and do as I say. We have a problem on our hands."

"What kind of problem?"

"I'll explain later." Fleta looked out the window. What could she tell her son? That a hundred Wichitas were going to be drunk and dangerous?

By mid-afternoon, the celebration grew louder beyond the wall. One by one the Osage women and children came to the house. Fleta served them tea. They sat quietly on the floor sipping the beverage, seemingly undisturbed by the revelry outside. But Fleta noticed the women did not giggle.

Beyond the stockade, drums grew louder and voices shriller. She could see her son's frustration at his confinement.

"What are they doing, Ma?" he asked plaintively.

"Celebrating."

"My friend Red Elk didn't ask me to come and celebrate," Luke complained.

Fleta shook her head in exasperation. "He wasn't allowed to. Theirs is a private celebration."

Fleta knew Luke was not satisfied by her answer, but fortunately he did not pressure her for any other information.

Outside, the chanting and shouts grew in intensity. She imagined a massacre. All her life she had heard of Indians who got drunk and then went on a killing rampage. And it was worse when they were sold bad whiskey, for it made them almost insane. She trembled at the thought of wild Indians barging in with tomahawks and knives. The blood pounded in her temples and cold sweat broke out on her neck.

Spotted Horse came in the front door. He took the Hawkins and the ammunition, then wordlessly exited again. The worried look on his granite face did nothing to reassure Fleta.

The sharp report of gunshots caused her to jump. The sounds came from the direction of the camp. "Dear God," she whispered, "don't let those wild people come in here. Oh, why did I ever leave Arkansas?" She looked at Luke seated on the pallet. Her mouth drawn in a tight line, she rose and went to search for a gun. Taking the pistol from the panniers, she walked to the rocker. If the Wichitas got past the Osages, at least she would have some protection.

Outside, the laughter and screams grew louder. Fleta rested the gun in her lap, then placed her hands over her ears, praying for Noble to come home.

In the darkness, Noble slipped along the horse line. Ahead of him, Rivers and No-Eyes were moving shadows. He heard a horse snort, and was certain it was not one of his own. When he and the two Indians reached the last pack horse, they crouched in council.

"Are they Indians?" Noble asked.

"White men," No-Eyes said flatly.

There was no time to question the brave; he was probably right. Rivers had the double action .30 revolver that Noble had carried to Arkansas. Noble reached out and stopped No-Eyes. "Here, take this pistol." He offered one of his Colts. "Shoot carefully."

The Wichita nodded and moved to the right. Rivers went to the left. Noble unbuttoned his coat and felt the night air invade his shirt when he drew out the other single action .36 from his belt.

Something howled and Noble wondered if it was a wolf or a man. He moved ahead carefully, knowing instinctively that whoever was out there was not friendly. He crept down the ridge, the re-frozen ground crunching under his boot soles. His eyes searched for any movement as he cautiously proceeded. He shrugged off his concern and began to hurry in a bent-over trot.

A pistol rang out to his right. No-Eyes' pistol belched more flame and smoke. The fight was on. But where in the hell was the enemy?

Noble's question was answered at the sound of boots heels and a figure came running toward him. A glimpse of the hat told Noble this was no Indian. The Colt barked in Noble's fist. The intruder snapped back a wild shot to the side of Noble. The shooter was close to a dark line of head high bushes when Rivers fired his pistol. The figure halted, obviously hard hit. Noble heard his rifle clatter to the ground.

No-Eyes joined him and they rushed down the hillside together. Were there others?

"Get to the horses!" someone ordered.

Noble recognized the voice.

"Damn Injuns got Red!" another voice shouted.

"Shut up and ride," Izer Goodman ordered.

"You low-life bastard!" Noble swore, crashing through the bushes in pursuit. He realized it was futile when he heard horse hooves pounding off into the night. Regardlessly, Noble emptied his pistol into the inky darkness after them.

Rivers joined him as he stood in the chest high brambles.

"Izer Goodman," Noble said in disgust.

"Yes," the Osage said.

Both men turned to the screams from above them on the hill.

"The squaws found him," Rivers said.

"Red Barber," Noble said to himself. The war cries of the

squaws were worse than the wolves' howls. He pushed back to camp to reload his pistol, not wishing to be a part of Barber's mutilation.

The continuing screams of their grisly attack on the outlaw made Noble sick to his stomach. At least Fleta and Luke were safe. As for Izer, he would get that bully bastard. Noble had a big score to settle with Goodman and Dawson.

Dawn was a pink streak when Noble completed saddling his horse. The stark, naked corpse of Red Barber lay on the blood mottled snow, thirty feet from the picket line. Brutally scalped, his genitals were stuffed in his mouth. Noble turned his back on the nauseating sight. Spotted Horse's weather forecast was running out. They needed to be back at the fort by dark; the heavy-laden horses were becoming too weary to plow much more snow.

They rode southwest. Mid-day, Noble spotted the column of smoke rising against the sky. He turned back to Rivers, riding behind him.

"Is that the fort?"

The Osage peered keenly at the smoke in the flat distance. He nodded, his brown eyes troubled.

"I'm going ahead," Noble said decisively. "Bring all our horses, but come slowly, for they're tired."

Rivers agreed. Noble pounded the gray with his heels. The great horse responded, but Noble felt saddened for even the gray had been pushed too hard. Hooves splashed the thawed ground and Noble strained forward. Miles of rotten snow swept beneath the lathered horse's dripping belly.

If Goodman had harmed Fleta, Noble vowed, he would castrate the bastard.

Finally he could see the picketed wall. The smoke appeared to be coming from beyond it. Perhaps the Wichita camp. He drew the gray to a walk, wondering what had happened.

When he rode up the last grade, he saw Spotted Horse and Barge standing in the gate with their rifles.

"What's on fire?" he demanded as he quickly dismounted the heaving horse.

"The Wichita camp. Their tepees."

"Why?"

Spotted Horse shook his head in disgust. "Crazy drunk. Izer sold them four barrels of whiskey."

"That bastard! Are the Wichitas all right?"

Spotted Horse grinned. "Bad sick, no tepees. But they will live."

Then Noble saw Fleta. She ran forward and launched herself into his outstretched arms.

"I was sure worried when I saw the smoke," Noble said, holding her tightly against his chest.

"Thank Spotted Horse, he kept all of us safe." She wanted Noble for herself, for them to be alone. She hoped he never left her again for so long.

"We're rich," he whispered. "Richer than I ever imagined. We've got enough to stock your store and the Wichitas got so many goods, their horses are swayed back. But Lord deliver me from ever taking three squaws shopping again," he said, heady with their reunion.

"What happened?"

"Let's go inside. I'm starved for your cooking. I'll tell you all about it. Why, I've got enough peppermint candy to make Luke and all the Osages sick."

Fleta looked a his tired face and knew he wasn't telling her everything. "What's wrong?"

He stopped and looked at her, surprised that she read him so easily. He peered beyond the gates in the direction of the Indian Territory.

"I was just wondering where that bastard Goodman is now."

"Come on. Don't worry about him, he's not around here." She urged him toward the house and shivered when a wave of unexplained apprehension washed over her.

Before spring, Noble vowed, he was going to give Izer Goodman what he deserved.

Chapter Five

Fleta stood with her hands on her hips, surveying the piles of goods stacked to the ceiling of her house.

What had Noble said? That there would be time to sort it out later? He had left early that morning to find some timber. She shook her head; Noble McCurtain was a man full of plans and schemes. They appeared to hatch with each day. Strangely enough, they were successful so far, but tying him down to setting up a store would be impossible.

A ledger book, ink and a pen set were among the supplies. Before he left, Noble hastily showed her the blurry invoices from Patterson's Mercantile. "Just set up a book, substract sales and..." Fleta shook her head at recalling his words. "...you'll know what to record." That was easy for him to say.

There were bolts of material, dried beans, flour sacks, baking powder, dried apples, horse shoe nails, and cigars. Why cigars? she asked herself as she skimmed down the crumpled pages. Iron pans, four shovels. She raised her eyes to check for the tools. They were leaning against the far wall. Thread, needles, scissors, pins, buttons and candy. Fleta stared in disbelief at the piles of merchandise. Would she ever get this mess sorted out and put it in some kind of order?

What hadn't he bought? Probably something the first customer would ask for. Determined, she made up her mind there was going to be some order to this madness.

Mannah entered the store. Fleta smiled and gestured at the piles of goods.

"Have you ever seen so much stuff?" she asked. When Mannah shrugged her shoulders, Fleta made an instant decision. The Indian was going to learn the store business.

"Mannah, how would you like to be a clerk?"

Mannah looked at her with puzzlement. She shook her head as if to say that she did not comprehend what Fleta was saying.

"Don't worry about it. You and I are going to run this store."

Mannah managed a bemused nod.

"First, we have to put all the material bolts over there," Fleta explained, pointing to her right. "That means we'll have to get a lot of stuff out of the way. You understand?" Mannah shrugged, but smiled her willingness to please Fleta.

A few hours later, both women were holding their lower backs and wearing tired smiles.

"Store business lot of work," Mannah said, amused.

Fleta agreed, but the woman was going to work out fine as a helper. She was a quick learner and in time would be a big asset.

Both women turned when the door was flung open. Two very tall Wichita men entered, arms folded over their chests, eagle feathers brushing the top of the doorway as they passed through.

Fleta watched as they surveyed the room, then looked at Mannah. Their words meant nothing to Fleta, but they obviously wanted something.

Fortunately Mannah seemed to understand them. She nodded. "How much pay for two cigars?" she asked Fleta.

Fleta blinked at the thought of Indians wanting cigars. "I'll have to look at the invoices."

The Wichitas spoke again with Mannah. Fleta's fingers were clumsy as she ruffled through the invoices. Where was the cost of those blasted cigars? Finally she found the price. One box cost a dollar.

"What will he give?" Fleta whispered to Mannah.

Fleta watched carefully as Mannah spoke and used sign language to get her question across. Finally she turned to Fleta with a smile.

"They say—one pelt for two cigars."

"Fine," Fleta said quickly. Any fur was worth more than five cents.

"Good," Mannah said with a conspiratorial smile. "They

will think they have out traded us by getting two for one.''

Mannah made more signs, but the bargainer shook his head. After a few more moments of haggling, one of the men shouted to a woman who was stationed outside the open door. She came in, carrying a prime wolf hide that shone like silk. But Mannah did not accept it without examining every inch of the fur, then she turned and tried to open the cigar box.

Fleta hurriedly found a knife on her dry sink and used it to scratch open the seal and pry back the fine wooden, hinged top of the box. A heavy aroma of rich tobacco filled her nostrils.

Her very first sale. Who would have ever thought about trading cigars for furs. A smile crossed her face as the two men left, sniffing the length of the cigars. Obviously, Noble thought of such a trade. A feeling of warmth hugged Fleta as if he was there himself. She glanced around with satisfaction at her house piled ceiling high with smelly yard goods, crates of items, leaving only narrow paths to walk. Fleta felt confident. Oh, Noble McCurtain, I do love you.

Miles south, River and Barge were helping Noble saw down several small trees with a crosscut saw. The new hat shading his eyes was becoming a familiar feature on his head.

Satisfied they had enough wood for the younger oxen to pull, Noble chained the larger load to the mature oxen's yoke. When he spoke to them the teams began to shoulder the load, Noble exchanged a confident smile with the Osages.

''Let's go home,'' he said stepping into the gray's stirrup.

Barge shouldered the great saw and the blade made a warping sound that amused both Indians. Noble shouted at the steers to keep walking. The experience he had gained by driving his uncle's steers and freighting was not wasted.

Now he needed an Illinois plow to cut the prairie. A dozen furrows would make a fire break. Prairie fires could be a deadly force, scorching everything for miles. A wide band devoid of vegetation would save the fort. Yes, he definitely needed a plow.

March came with warm south winds, but winter returned intermittently to the plains with hard frosts and light snow. The Wichitas were sober and ready to move back south to the Indian Territory. They packed up camp, but before they left, Chief Tall Timber rode inside the fort to speak to Noble. His horse was gaudy with painted symbols and feathers braided in his mane.

"You are a good man, Noble McCurtain. We will return if the 'blue pants' will let us come. No white man has treated us so well.

"The whiskey was very bad. If we find this man, Izer Goodman, we will send him to his gods. No-Eyes wants to kill him slowly for his woman burned his lodge while he was gone and No-Eyes cannot forget sleeping all winter under a buffalo robe."

"Come again, Chief," Noble said. "The Wichitas are welcome in my camp." He watched the man turn and ride out the gate.

"Good thing they're leaving," Fleta said softly from behind him.

"Why is that, Mrs. McCurtain?" Noble asked, turning and putting his hands on her hips.

"Because I'm nearly out of cigars." She and Noble both laughed.

During the next days, Noble busied himself repairing the stables with the posts they had dragged back. Spotted Horse seemed uneasy and made frequent trips on horseback out of the fort. Noble wondered what the Osage was looking for, but decided the man would tell him when he was ready.

One afternoon in early April, Spotted Horse rode up to where Noble and Rivers were working. He slipped to the ground and announced, "The main herd is coming."

"Main herd?" Noble echoed with a frown.

"The buffalo returns."

"Is that important?" Noble asked, tilting back his hat so he could see the man better.

"A long time ago, a medicine man said, when the buffalo no longer returns, the Osage will be gone."

"So that's what had you worried. You were afraid they weren't coming back?"

Spotted Horse nodded. "So few Osage now. When we are gone, who will hunt the buffalo?"

"Probably white men," Noble said.

"Then everyone will have a day. Next, the white man will come more than the buffalo."

"I reckon so," Noble said soberly. He considered the Osage, he looked like a man who wanted to surrender but there was no one to accept him.

Streams of wagons came by in late April. Folks were bubbling with the news. "War's about over! They got Lee hemmed in the Wilderness. It'll all be over in a few days."

Wagons meant commerce. Folks forgot necessities, things they needed or coveted. The Osage sold their tanned buffalo hides to be used for leather repairs. Noble recalled one man's jubilation as he told them about where he was going. "Jefferson Territory is the place to go. Richer than a yard up a bull's ass. Land's so rich, pumpkins grow to wagon size. You better leave this wind blessed prairie and go along with us."

Noble suppressed his amusement. He had seen that country at the base of the Rocky Mountains when he was freighting. Folks had said that same thing in Illinois about Missouri, chasing riches they just couldn't grasp. But Noble was not about to burst their dreams. His steadily declining store stock and rising profits pleased him more than any big pumpkin, even a wagon sized one.

"I'm going to send Rivers to Independence with an order for more supplies. Patterson's can send a freighter down with it."

"Good idea," Fleta smiled as she looked up from her book-keeping. "But will he go?"

"He may ride a horse in the ground to get there, then not stay a minute longer than he has to. But I think he'll carry an order up there for me."

Noble was not surprised at the shortness of the Osage's round trip. He read the letter Rivers had brought back.

Dear Noble,

Thank you for your order. It is always a pleasure doing business with your firm. While prices are higher now than they were this past winter, perhaps now the war is over, we shall see a more stable economy.

A dependable freight company will deliver your goods in a week or two, depending on weather conditions.

Hope to see you again in person.

Sincerely yours,
Cedric and Alex Patterson

"What should we call our 'firm'?" Fleta asked after Noble finished reading the letter to her.

"Western Kansas Mercantile?" he suggested, smiling down in her face.

"No, that will never do." She steered him out of the store onto the porch. "Why not simply call it the Great Western Company?"

"Sounds kinda grand for a little cabin with a high wall around it."

"You don't see it do you?" she teased.

"What?" he asked, frowning.

"The great business that will grow here?"

Noble felt his face heat up. "You're picking on me."

"No, I'm not," she said, her face sober. "I can see, Noble. You're the dangdest builder I've ever known."

Noble just stood there and savored the kiss she planted on his cheek. She was right. He did intend to have a big business. Some day.

The freighter arrived two weeks later in the form of a double set of wagons behind several span of oxen. The driver-owner wore knee high boots and spat a wad of tobacco as he stomped through the gate.

"Gawdamn, man," the bull whacker swore with a look around the fort. "Why you got a regular place here. I thought this belonged to the Haskins Docking Company."

"They abandoned it."

"Well, when they hear that you're doing this kind of business, they'll be out here to claim it."

Noble nodded. He must send a letter back with this man for the Pattersons. Surely they knew a lawyer who would settle his claim on the land. There had to be a way to prove his ownership.

The man poked Noble with a thumb. "You let them redskins sleep in here?"

"They're Osage."

"Savages. All the red bastards should be shot. Now the war's over, we'll get busy on that."

"Is it really over?" Noble asked, not satisfied with the rumors of the surrender.

"Damn sure is." The man punctuated his speech by spitting. "Lee hung up his sword. Give it to Grant at Apple something in Virginny."

"Good," Noble said absently. He looked away, impatient to get away from the loud mouthed, irritating man.

"Hell, yes. Now I'll have work. Them bluebellies are gonna raise hell with those red devils. Going to put up a bunch of forts so settlers won't be molested by them. Maybe we'll get us a president who'll put a bounty on their red skins." He spit contemptuously. "Hell, I'll do it for free."

"Well, don't plan on starting anything here," Noble warned him with a cold glare. "These people are mine. Don't even think about harming them."

"You some kinda damn Injun lover?"

Noble's eyes glittered with cold rage as he stared down the man. "You're damned right and don't you forget it." He turned on his heel, too furious to add anything else. He wanted to hurry and unload the supplies and get the damned Indian hater on his way as quickly as possible. A shudder of anger rippled through him as he stalked inside the store.

Fleta noticed his face looked like a thundercloud. "Noble, what's wrong?" she asked quietly.

"Nothing!" Noble gritted his teeth to control his boiling wrath. He took a deep breath and stood rigid until he had his rage fully under control.

"Why are you so wrought up?"

"It's nothing. That freighter just made me angry," he said, dismissing her concerns.

"Why?"

"We'll talk later," he promised.

Noble involved himself in unloading the freight. The driver's men even seemed to resent the Indians so Noble stayed in the center of the activity. He was not about to allow any of the men to abuse his charges.

With the furs loaded to go back for Patterson's, Noble was relieved when the freighter pulled out to camp beyond the fort's walls.

Noble stood on the porch, his eye squinted to watch them move on.

"I've never seen you so furious," Fleta said, when she joined him on the porch.

"Hogan—that's his name—is an Indian hater."

"So? Lots of people in the west are."

"I guess you're right. I just realized how much those kind of people bother me."

"Remember how uneasy I was at first around them? Now Mannah and I are close friends."

Noble looked at her keenly then sighed. "You're right."

She smiled and looked at him with a twinkle in her eyes, wanting to lighten his mood. "Will my rich husband want to trade me for some grand lady when he gets richer?"

"What?"

"I'm perfectly serious, Noble." The mischief in her eyes belied her statement. She watched a grin curve his lips with satisfaction.

"I have you, Fleta. What more could I want?"

"You say that now. But what about when you're rich and famous?"

"Don't be silly," he said curtly.

Fleta accepted his rebuke, noting that all of his anger had not dissipated. Obviously now was not the time to be flippant with him.

May was stormy, but wagons and riders kept coming, making stops at the store. Busy rolling up a bolt of cloth, Fleta looked up when a figure ducked inside the door. He was very tall and carried a black stovepipe hat in his hand. With a gasp of shock, Fleta recognized his gaunt face. The minister from her home town in Wesley, Arkansas.

"Reverend Jordan!"

The dark frown on his face was foreboding. "Mrs.—"

"Mrs. McCurtain," she inserted quickly.

He shook his head and clucked his teeth. "Oh no, this is a terrible error. Your husband, Wilbourne Corey, has just returned home. He thinks you're dead."

Fleta felt her knees buckle. Only the reverend's sinewy arms saved her from falling.

Mannah rushed in, upon seeing the tall man bent over Fleta, grabbed the muzzle loader and aimed it threateningly at the minister.

"Get back!" Mannah ordered.

"I'm a man of God," he protested. "She merely fainted."

46

Fleta weakly asserted herself. "It—it's all right, Mannah." She jerked from Jordan's grasp and pushed herself up to her feet.

"My dear woman, I know this has been a shock, but you must return immediately to Arkansas. Your poor husband needs to know you're alive."

Noble burst in the room. Having recognized Jordan's silhouette as he had approached, Noble sprinted the gray to reach the store. Fearing the reverend's motives for coming, Noble's face was lined with concern. Fleta's pale face and visibly trembling hands confirmed his suspicions.

"Fleta, are you all right? What's going on?" he asked, crossing to her side and placing a protective arm across her shoulders.

"Oh, Noble," she whispered looking at him helplessly, "Wilbourne's come home. He's alive."

Noble's first thought was, 'So what?' Corey had no claim on her. Fleta was his now and he intended to see that she stayed with him. He glared at Reverend Jordan, his eyes damning the man for meddling.

"I did not come here to upset her," the reverend said quietly. "In fact I had no idea this was your place. But there is the Christian—"

"What is it you need?" Noble cut him off before he could start preaching. They left Arkansas because of Jordan and his church elders scolding them for living together without the benefit of matrimony. Before Noble came, no one had offered to help feed her and the boy or cut fire wood and see to them. Would it have been more Christian for them to have starved?

"Perhaps some beans. The supplies I carry are meager."

Noble scooped some dried beans from the barrel into a poke. He handed the small canvas bag to the man.

"How much do I owe you?"

Noble shook his head. "Nothing. You can leave now."

The reverend sighed. "Very well. But I shall pray for your soul and that you and Mrs. Corey will do the right thing and save yourself from eternal damnation and the fires of hell."

"It's settled, Reverend," Noble said curtly. "Good day." He waited until he was sure that the man was mounted and on his way.

"Are you all right?" he asked her again.

"Yes, I'll be fine."

"I'll be outside if you need me." He was anxious to get away so he could think.

"Yes." The words came out so flatly that Noble found a stab of remorse.

In the sunshine, he leaned back against the fresh post he had used to resurrect the sagging stable.

Spotted Horse rode in and dismounted. "You sick, Noble?" the Osage asked.

"No. My wife's husband has returned from the war."

"He is here?" the Indian asked.

"No, no. He's at their old home in Arkansas."

Spotted Horse fell silent for a moment, his eyes stared at the plains as Noble's were doing. Then he spoke softly, "You speak of white man ways."

Noble studied the toes of his boots. "Her husband went to war for three winters. Now he's home. We thought he was dead."

"Three winters?" Spotted Horse shook his head, his braids flying around his shoulders, the eagle feather swaying in the wind. "Why so long?"

"He was fighting a war."

"Perhaps he is a ghost?"

"Maybe. He haunts me," Noble said aloud, but his thoughts were silent. She can't leave. He wondered how he would convince her to stay.

Having reached his own decision, Noble went back inside the store. He closed the door and leaned against it, not wanting any interruptions. For a moment he felt hopeless looking at her sad face.

"I'll have to go pack." Fleta's tear-filled words knifed him. Her swollen eyes and air of dejection summed up her torment. "Noble, I am legally his wife. There is nothing else to do but go back to him."

Noble was frustrated by his inability to do something to assert his rights. He and Fleta had accomplished a great deal together. Their business was thriving; they were building a future together. She couldn't possibly go back to Wilbourne!

He combed his fingers through his hair and frowned. "Fleta, what if...what if he won't accept you back?"

She sat on the rocker he had traded from a passing settler.

"Then I'll—" she broke off and burst into tears. Putting her hands to her face, she sobbed. "This is all my fault. I wanted you so badly that I sinned. I'm living in sin."

"No!" Noble rushed across the room and knelt in front of her. "This is no sin, Fleta. God didn't want you and Luke to starve. No kind of God wanted that. Damnation, Fleta! What we did was not wrong.

"Let him find another woman. He left you. If he really cared he would have come back before now. Fleta, I would never leave you like that. Kansas is our home now. Stay with me."

She drew her hands away from her wet face and looked at him pleadingly. "Noble, I don't know what to do."

"Stay here."

Numbly she slipped to her knees and fell into his arms. Her sorrow drenched his shoulder. They held each other for a long time. He knew their problem was not settled, but a firm resolve fermented in his mind. He would not give her up.

The next morning, Fleta was no closer to reaching a decision. She was tense, her nerves stretched tautly. When she dropped a cup and it shattered at her feet, she jumped back as though shot. Her favorite tea cup was in fragments at her feet. To her, it represented her peaceful, secure life with Noble.

Mannah stopped her as she bent to pick up the pieces.

"I will clean it up, Fleta. You are trembling so much you might cut yourself."

"Am I that bad?" she asked ruefully.

"Yes."

Fleta had grown very close to Mannah. The Indian woman was accepted by the white customers, and her skills with the Indians amazed Fleta. The Osage wife quickly learned arithmetic and a varied English vocabulary.

"You can never go home," Mannah said as she rose with the broken porcelain in her hand.

Fleta frowned. "What do you mean?"

"They will not accept you. Even the dogs will bite you. Your first man will wonder how you could have slept with another. He will question what the other man did to you. How it was with him. His jealous mind will go crazy. He will treat you as a used thing.

It will not be the same. Nothing is as it was. It will be very different.''

Fleta's upper teeth cut into her lower lip. Would Wilbourne act like that toward her? Perhaps he would be angry? How did Mannah know so much?

Then Fleta remembered Mannah was not an Osage. Had she returned to her own people one time and had the Indian camp dogs snipped at her heels?

Cold silence would be her sentence if she returned to Arkansas. Wilbourne would busy himself with his farming and expect his meals on time. He would snore at night and ignore her, except when he felt some urge. Then he would use her body to punish her for her sins. And he would be within a husband's rights.

Fleta closed her eyes and silently sorted out her options. God will have to forgive me. I couldn't stand such penance. No, Luke and I will have a better life with Noble. We will stay here with him.

She planned to tell Noble her decision to remain when he returned to the fort. Earlier, Spotted Horse reported an approaching wagon train, and Noble went to meet them. It was now his custom to ride ahead and greet the newcomers. He moved from wagon to wagon, shaking hands and extolling the store goods. He was very proficient at hawking their wares. Sometimes too good, she thought. Business would become so booming that at the end of the day she would collapse into a chair, drained of strength. How long would this new stream of customers be in the store? She wanted a few moments alone with Noble so she could tell him her decision. She looked out the small window and she wished he would hurry.

The gray acted frisky as they crossed the green waving grass. Noble was pleased he hadn't wind-broken the big horse by pushing him so hard returning from Independence. Truly this horse was the greatest Noble had ever owned. He must have cost the head bushwhacker, Captain Watson, a pretty penny.

Even in the early morning the May sun was building up heat. Meadowlarks whistled and quail conversed with their mates. In the distance the wagon hoops snaked toward Noble. He set the gelding into a rocking lope and rode toward the outriders in front of the line.

Colonel Rupert Lyons, a man with bearing and a white pointed beard, was the wagonmaster. He wore a deerskin outfit with enough quills and beads on it to make a squaw jealous. Noble guessed that Lyons might be more comfortable wearing a suit. There was a certain sophistication about the man that the frontier fringe could not hide.

"We've heard about you," the colonel said after Noble had introduced himself. "You're supposed to be the most honest merchant west of Missouri."

Noble thanked him and rode alongside the lead wagon. "We don't sell whiskey to settlers or to the Indians. We give the customers every consideration and courtesy."

Rupert nodded. "We'll camp at your fort tonight. You know how people are. Two weeks out and they figure they've forgot something. Guess that's why a store out here is good business."

"Reckon so," Noble said amiably. "If you don't mind, I'll ride back and speak to folks, tell them what we have. It saves time later."

"Of course." Rupert tilted his head back and studied Noble. "Wait," he said, reaching out a hand to still him. "Where did you get that hat?"

Noble grinned and pushed the brim up with his thumb. "In Independence. A man named Stetson made it in Philadelphia."

"That's some hat," the colonel said with admiration. "Would you consider selling it?"

Noble shook his head. "Afraid not. It was a gift." He turned and started down the line. Some of the folks were friendly. He shook hands, answered questions, bantered with them, and told them some of the things he had on hand at the store. Other members of the wagon train were sullen, suspicious and tight lipped. In the case of the latter, he would just smile and ride onto the next wagon.

Oxen powered most of the wagons. A few draft horse teams could be seen, but they were hard to slow to a steer's gait. And horses could not forage and live off the land the way the oxen could. Horses needed grain to work.

Noble approched a thin faced man walking beside his double team of oxen. A troubled look crossed the man's face as Noble rode closer. The man appeared to be growing angry.

"My gun, Mary! Get my gun!" the man shouted and bolted for

the wagon box. Noble read the bewilderment in the woman's expression. The settler dodged and ducked around the front wheel and tried to get the rifle away from her and out of the wagon.

"He's riding my gray horse!" he screamed. "That's my horse!"

Noble went cold at the man's words. He practically called him a horse thief. This gray was Captain Watson's horse—somehow he must talk sense into the man.

"Hold up!" Noble shouted, but the man wrenched the rifle from his wife's desperate grip. Noble's hand sought the butt of the Colt on his right hip. The settler staggered back and fired. The bullet plowed in the dust but caused the gray to rear on his hind feet.

"Give me the powder," the red faced man shouted to his pale faced wife. When she did not respond to his request, the man took the barrel in both hands and raised the stock to use as a club on Noble. He charged with a deep throated growl.

The Colt barked in Noble's hand. The bullet's impact slammed into the man, stopping him with sledge hammer force. The rifle fell, barely brushing Noble's stirrup as the wounded man's mask of anger melted and he collapsed to his knees.

The woman's shrill cry caused Noble's jaw to stiffen as he fought the excited grey.

The red flow through the man's fingers, clamped over his chest, told Noble the wound was serious. The woman stumbled and fell trying to come to her husband's aid; but she never reached him before he pitched face down and his legs kicked involuntarily in death's throes.

"You've killed him! Oh, my God, you've killed him," she screamed.

Others came rushing to the scene. Noble felt cold despite the sun's heat when one of the wagon leaders looked up from examining the man.

"Mister, he must have lost his mind. What the hell was wrong? Did he know you?"

Noble shook his head. "No."

"Nat Gunter was a bitter man, but he had no call to attack you."

The man's words were small comfort, Noble was still uncertain about the mood of the crowd. He gave the man a grateful nod.

"What happened?" someone called out.

"Gunter went crazy and shot at this man," the witness repeated.

The colonel and his scouts came rushing in. The entire wagon train was in disarray. Noble dismounted and spoke to a few people in the edge of the crowd.

The wagonmaster waded in while two of his hard eyed employees sat their horses. Noble felt their eyes size him up.

Rupert emerged from the gathering. "He thought you had stolen his gray horse."

Noble shook his head. "I bought this one in Arkansas."

"Well, Gunter obviously thought you had stolen him."

"Where was he from?" Noble asked.

"Missouri, somewhere."

"I'm sorry, sir, for the trouble," Noble apologized. "But he shot at me without warning and then attacked me with the rifle." Noble felt queasy. Watson might have stolen him or even bought the horse from a thief. "I never stole this horse, Colonel," Noble added with a direct look.

"Oh, I believe you. He just went mad when he saw that horse. times have been hard on people because of the war."

Noble agreed. The widow's sobbing was burned his ears. "Tell her I'm sorry."

"I will," the wagonmaster promised. He turned to the people. "Everyone, get to their wagons. There's no more we can do here. Joe, Leonard, you take care of the body for Mrs. Gunter. We're going on. Nothing more we can do."

Noble rode back to the fort, his thoughts blighted by the shooting. Even a flushed prairie chicken did not raise his spirits. He questioned himself ruthlesly. Had he shot too quickly? Why hadn't he just driven the gray into the man? How could he know someone stole the gray? But the vision of the man's blood seeping through his fingers and his desperate wife crawling toward him would not go away.

Deeply depressed, Noble rode through the fort gate. He raised his eyes when Fleta came outside in a new dress that was as blue as her eyes.

Noble's heart began to hammer, then stilled to nearly a stop. She was leaving.

"Noble, what's wrong?" she asked, seeing the stricken look on his face.

He dismounted with leaden boots, swept his hat off, and mopped the perspiration from his brow on his sleeve. "It's been a bad day and I have a feeling it just got worse." He issued a great sigh.

"Noble...I've decide to stay," she said quietly, her eyes downcast.

"What?" Noble jerked his head up and willed her to look at him.

"Aren't you pleased?" she asked.

"Lord, yes!" He rushed forward and swept her into his arms. His mouth pressed against her hair and face, his strong arms crushed her to him.

Fleta almost laughed at his reckless abandon. His guns were digging into her stomach and his passionate caresses were almost obscene. She was Fleta McCurtain, God forgive her. If He would.

Chapter Six

In June, 1865, a new kind of train came out of the Indian Territory, one made of longhorn cattle as far as the eye could see.

"Wonder where those cattle are headed?" Noble asked Spotted Horse. The two men squatted on a gentle rise, watching the approaching longhorns.

"Plenty of them," Spotted Horse said.

The two men rode out earlier that morning to meet the cattle drivers. Before he left, Noble called on the two Osage men he had come to rely on. Rivers and Barge, armed with rifles, listened to his instructions on guarding the fort.

Noble had little reason to suspect problems. According to Spotted Horse, no other wagons were coming. The Osage chief spent most of his days searching for prospective customers or troublemakers—a job he took very seriously.

Fortunately, since they did not sell whisky, few of the riff-raff type came by the store. Temperance was a new word to Noble, and it impressed and surprised his customers.

A haze of dust lifted, churned up by thousands of hooves coming behind the giant lead steer with his jangling bell. Cowboys rode on either side of the trail-broken cattle. Amidst bawling, dust and shouts, the line of longhorns snaked north.

Two wagons with sun-cured yellow tops paralleled the stream. A separate large herd of saddle stock was being driven behind the wagons.

Noble set the gray toward a man shouting directions.

Politely, he and Spotted Horse stopped short and waited for the man to ride over to them.

"Howdy," the tall man greeted them. His tanned face held a down-to-earth honesty which Noble respected.

"Howdy, I'm Noble McCurtain and this is Spotted Horse. We have a trading post about a day's drive north of here."

"Am I about out of Indian Territory?"

"Yes, you're probably in Kansas now." Noble smiled at the man's heartfelt sigh of relief.

"Well, thank God for that. I'm Toby Evans from Fort Worth, Texas." He extended a calloused hand for them to shake. "Glad to meet you two. I'm sorry, Spotted Horse, but I've paid more tributes to Indians than I ever knew existed. We're headed for Independence, Missouri. Can I make it, you reckon?"

"Certainly, but it'll take you a month," Noble informed him.

"Hell, I ain't got nothing but time. Steers are worth ten cents in Texas."

"A pound?" Noble asked.

"Gawd, no! A head."

Noble did a quick calculation. "Do you own all of these cattle?"

Evans shook his head. "If I had that much money, I'd never have made this drive in the first place."

"At the price of beef in Independence, I figure you'll make another drive," Noble said wryly.

The man's eyes lit up with anticipation. "Really?" He pounded his large saddle, his sun-squinted eyes surveying the cattle. Noble knew what the man was thinking about. Money. In his high crown hat, gun low on his slim hips, Toby Evans was about to become a man of means.

"McCurtain?" Toby asked, stretching his shoulders back. "I have a bunch of tail enders, road sore ones, heifers heavy with calves. Odds and ends. You wouldn't be interested in swapping them for supplies, would you?"

"How much for them?" Noble asked. He tried to appear indifferent.

"They ain't worth much to me," Evans said. "Say, fifty-cents a head."

Noble knew his answer before the man had even spoken. Big steers could be broken and used to replace the oxen. Broken to a yoke, they would be worth forty or fifty dollars a team. Cows would beget more. While the steers were still sore footed from the long drive, he could easily break them. "All right, Evans. You got a deal," he said with a grin. He reached out and shook hands with the man, sealing their bargain.

"Good enough, McCurtain. We'll need supplies. Flour and beans, a few other essentials."

"You keep going north." Noble pointed. "You can't miss our place."

The men parted. Noble and Spotted Horse headed back to the fort. He was sure the Osage would not be as pleased as he was about the purchase of the cattle. The bucks considered oxen rather dull and stupid, but they would help him break them.

Noble was busy considering his new venture when Spotted Horse broke his concentration.

"Now you need a son."

He almost reined in the gray. A picture of his freighting days came vividly to mind at the Indian's words. He'd been sick and thought he might be dying. His affliction was called mumps. Out of his head with fever, his swollen throat was nearly shut. His testicles were so enlarged that every time the wagon swayed, he felt them torn apart. Noble fought the germ for days by working until he collapsed beside the team. His boss, Ben Rutherford, and a couple other men carried him to a pallet in the wagon, where an army doctor examined him. The physician shook his head, saying, "You're fever's breaking. The swelling will go down, but I don't reckon you'll ever sire any offspring. Sorry son."

"What?" Noble asked, trying to focus on the man's face. What did the doctor mean?

"You'll be all right, but men that get mumps like this, can't have children."

"Oh." Noble had almost fainted from exhaustion and fever.

From somewhere far away, he heard Ben Rutherford's laugh. "Hell, boy, you'll live. Damned lucky. I figured you'd bust and die."

That episode in his life had been buried deeply beneath his subconscious; he hadn't thought about it for years, but Spotted Horse's comment about a son brought the scene back sharply. Noble studied the sea of grass and shook his head sadly. Someday he'd tell Fleta, but not now. She might feel he wasn't worthy and leave him. Her first man was whole. Luke was living proof of that fact.

He motioned to Spotted Horse and they short loped across the open country.

Later that evening when Noble told Fleta of his recent purchases, she looked at him with slight exasperation. "How many cattle did you get?"

"Fifty or so. We'll have oxen to sell next year..." He pulled her into his arms, smiling down at her frowning face.

"Noble, what are you doing?"

"Hugging my wife," he said with a laugh. "I'm glad to be home." He shurgged away his guilty secret.

"Let me put out the lamp," she whispered as she wriggled out of his hold. She blew out the lamp on a deep sigh of contentment. A warm glow engulfed her. She liked him this way.

Luke was fascinated with the Texas cowboys. After they made their trade with Noble and went on their way, minus the traded cattle, Luke tried to copy their style of dress. He wore a red neckerchief his mother made him and stuffed the cuffs of his pants into his buckskin boots.

Spotted Horse furnished him a pinto pony that soon learned to come to sliding stops in front of the house, then spin around on his hind legs with enough dust swirling to enrage Fleta.

"Luke McCurtain, take that pony out of this yard. Now!" She pointed to the gate.

The boy put his heels to the pinto's ribs and the pair tore out of the gate.

When Luke wasn't busy with school lessons, he was riding the horse the drawling cowboys had christened 'Shaw'.

Luke wondered what the Texans meant when they said, "Shaw, he's big enough for you." But his mind didn't linger long on any one thing, certainly not his mother's schooling or his chores.

The only thing he concentrated on was riding harder and faster.

His one other obsession was learning to twirl a lariat. His feet-tangling attempts drew scowls and laughter from the Osage and his family, but Luke was determined to master the rope.

On horseback, he chased the timid cottontails outside the fort. Darting and dashing around on Shaw, Luke regretted that his friend, Red Elk, wasn't there to join him. When the Wichitas returned, he and Red Elk would be two dust devils.

As the days warmed into summer, Luke's skill grew. Aided by a rope tied to his saddle horn, he rode standing up on the pony's back at a full gallop on the east-west wagon trail. A few spills only drove him to be more proficient.

Rivers showed him how to ride Indian style over the side and shoot at make believe enemies from beneath Shaw's neck. The Osage laughed when Luke spilled end-over-end into the grass while practicing the trick.

After one of his spills, Noble paused to grin at the boy who was up in a moment, chasing after the wild-maned pony.

Noble and Barge were busy with a Texas steer, trying to tame it to a yoke. The long horned steer was very snorty and occupied both men's attention.

Luke found the Texas cattle short-tempered compared to the dull oxen. "Noble," he asked on day, "can you train a steer to ride like a horse?"

Noble took a long look at the boy. He seemed to be growing so fast. A smile flickered across Noble's mouth as he drawled, "Well, Luke, I don't know. I've never seen it done." He hid a grin at the boy's impatient race to grow up. Luke had become a real son to him. The only son he would ever have.

"Can I try it?" Luke asked.

Noble shook his head to clear his troubled thoughts. "Sure, but why would you want to?"

"Well, if no one's ever done it before, then I could say I was the first."

"Well, that's a notion. It won't be easy," Noble cautioned him.

"I sort of figured that already," Luke nodded with a serious frown.

Luke found the yearling longhorn that Noble had cut out for him. The yearling was treacherous, butting and kicking frequently for the first two weeks that Luke haltered him.

That evening, with his chin resting on his hands, Luke looked out from his bed in the loft. His mother's voice caught his attention.

"That stupid bull is going to hurt Luke," Fleta said.

"Now, Fleta, the boy's got his mind set on breaking him to ride. Besides, he ain't a bull."

A smile spread across Luke's face. He was proud and pleased Noble believed in him enough to stand up to his mother. Was his real Pa as good a man as Noble McCurtain, he wondered. He'd overheard his mother and Noble talking about Wilbourne Corey. Maybe he'd just ride that steer to Arkansas and see him some day.

He'd miss Noble and the Osage if he went. They were good pals, nearly as good as the cowboys. Someday, he'd be a trail boss like Toby Evans and drive a thousand steers north.

By September, Luke had made a lot of progress with his yearling. He still tossed his horns which had grown from knobby stubs to six inches of dangerous weapons, but the steer no longer butted his master. The yearling could be saddled and even ridden, but his directions were poor when Luke pulled on the reins. He also would lay down and rise on command. Christened with an assortment of names—Fort Worthless, Cowboy, Tex, and few curse words—the steer eventually came to be called Tex.

Two men dressed in long canvas coats and good hats rode in one day while Luke was schooling Tex. They paused to watch him. He tapped on the ox's front leg. "Down," he commanded. The steer responded and lay down.

The taller of the two bearded riders dismounted and walked around Luke as he mounted the saddle.

"Quite a rig you have there, young man," he commented with a friendly smile.

"Yes, sir," Luke answered, impressed that the men were business men—not the run of the mill sort that usually came by. Both men were armed and had rifles in their saddle boots.

"Why, Jesse, if you had one of those, a posse could never track you," the other man said with a laugh.

"Posse," Luke echoed. The word was new to him. He wondered what it meant.

The friendly man tousled Luke's hair. "A posse is something bad that you don't want after you."

"Come on," the bigger man on horseback urged, "He's better off breaking steers to ride than being in our line of business."

The two men stopped at the store and bought supplies. They paid cash for their purchases then rode quietly on.

Spotted Horse, Luke noted, had been around the corner, acting disinterested. Luke knew better. The Osage only acted casual like that when he was suspicious. Later Luke overheard the Indian's conversation with Noble.

"They called themselves Jesse and Frank."

"They talked about a posse," Luke inserted helpfully.

"My God," Noble said with a shake of his head. "That was Frank and Jesse James. They're train robbers!"

"Really?" Luke's eyes danced with excitement. He tried to recall every word the men had said.

"Whoa, young man," Noble warned, seeing the look on his son's face. "Don't go fretting your mother about this. This is our secret."

Luke read the grim expression on Noble's face. "Yes, sir," he said with a sigh of disappointment. He had a new word, 'posse', and he couldn't even tell his mother. It seemed silly, but he instinctively read the manly look Noble gave him. He guessed some things were not for women to know.

He sat through supper uncharacteristically quiet. His mother babbled about the polite gentlemen who came by earlier. Luke squirmed in his seat, clamping his lips together to stop himself from speaking.

"They were very understanding," Fleta said, "when I explained we didn't sell whiskey because of our Indian trade."

Luke quickly finished his meal, wanting to get away to figure out something. A few minutes later, he sat on the front porch deep in thought. He decided that outlaws who tipped their hats and were very polite must not be very mean. Cowboys had manners like that, but from what he heard, outlaws didn't give a dang about manners and such.

His mother accused him of acting like an outlaw when he forgot his manners. Oh well, he reckoned she didn't know much about crooks anyway.

Chapter Seven

During the hot, cloudless days of September, Noble worried about the threat of a prairie fire. The grass was dry as tinder and the charred scars around the stockade told of past fires.

Two teams of oxen were hitched to a steel plow Noble traded from a passerby. He was ready to cut his fire-breaking furrows. As he worked under the grilling sun, sweat saturated his clothing. His temper was not improved any by the dull oxen's laborious movements. The plow's effort provided a few shallow scratches in the hard earth.

"Whoa!" Noble halted the team, then raised his Stetson with his thumb to survey his progress. He frowned at the strange-looking black man who rode up and was silently watching him.

As the man came nearer, Noble studied him. He was a bare-chested and huge. He rode a floppy-eared mule that wore a woman's straw hat. Noble blinked the sweat out of his eyes, wondering if he was seeing a mirage.

"Good day," the black man greeted him. Up close, his skin was coal black and the muscles bulged in his arms. He studied Noble's handiwork and pursed his lips. "Mister, you seem to be having trouble with your plowing," he observed.

Irritated already, Noble gave the giant a scowl. "Well, get off that silly mule and show me how to do it right," he said dryly.

"Me?" the man asked, searching around as if Noble had addressed some one else.

"You're the only one I see."

"Yes, sir." The man grinned and dismounted. Barefooted, his splayed toes were white with dust. In a few giant strides, he righted the plow as if it were a toy.

"Gittup!" he spoke sharply to the teams and used the force of his huge shoulders to drown the plow share through the centuries of roots. The chain grew taut, the oxen strained, and the once unyielding prairie sod fell dirt side up in a lengthening perfect furrow.

Noble removed his hat and scratched his head in amazement. Rivers came over and examined the furrow. Luke rode his pony back and forth in the fresh shallow trench.

Whoever he was, Noble decided, this man was no stranger to plowing. His voice boomed out a hymn about Jesus, the sound attracting Fleta and Osage women to the gate to investigate.

When he came back plowing the outside, the man introduced himself with a smile that exposed large white teeth. "Sudan Wilson."

"Noble McCurtain. Come, we'll have some lunch. My oxen are not used to work like that."

"You're a good man, Noble McCurtain."

A little taken back, Noble frowned. He looked at the man as they walked toward the store. "Why do you say that?"

"Cause," the man laughed openly. "I was so hungry I was thinking about eating them oxen out there."

Both men laughed as they entered the fort. Noble felt confident that the black man could contribute something useful to the fort's growing population.

Noble did notice the man's uneasiness eating at the table with him. "Eat up," Noble encouraged him. "We have plenty of food."

Sudan paused and set his spoon down. "I sure wouldn't want not to be invited back to supper." His wide eyes checked all of them.

Fleta chuckled and the others joined in her laughter. "Sudan Wilson, you eat all that you want. I'll fix more for supper."

"Yes ma'am." Sudan smiled and resumed spooning more stew in his mouth.

Noble exchanged a private nod of approval with his wife. "Well, Sudan. What else can you do besides plow?"

"Blacksmith. I can shoe horses, make hinges. I'm a fair wood worker and..." Sudan stopped and looked directly at Luke, "...and I can sure eat a lot."

"Why are you so black?" Luke asked.

"Cause I was borned that way," Sudan said with a good natured smile.

"Oh," the boy said and nodded his acceptance.

Relieved that the man was not offended, Noble smiled at Fleta. Everything would be all right.

Noble hired Sudan Wilson for twenty dollars a month plus food. Then he sent for coal, an anvil, a forge and supplies which came by freighter in October. The first frosts of fall gripped the plains in an icy coat.

Sudan lived in a tepee that the Osage women made for him. He decorated the sides with his own hand printed pictures. Noble took the greatest pride in Sudan's handiwork when the black man coerced all the men to strain their backs and rehang the long discarded gates. Noble stood back and watched them swing open and closed, satisfied the time might come when they needed their protection.

In the afternoon, he stood watching Sudan shoe the gray horse. He squatted as the big man bent over applying the new plates.

"You ever make a branding iron?" he asked curiously.

"Sure. How you want it made?"

"An M with little curls on the bottom of the outside legs," Noble said.

Sudan stood up and flexed his muscular back. "You better draw it, 'cause my schooling sure ain't much."

"Okay." Noble drew the design in the dust with a small stick.

"I'll make you two irons," Sudan said, studying the design in the dirt. "One'll be heating up while you're using the other one."

"Good idea," Noble said with approval.

Besides the irons, Sudan built Fleta a double bed. The bright rope lacing was tight as fiddle strings. She and Noble spent their first night in a real bed instead of a pallet on the floor. The early part of the evening was filled with suppressed laughs at the creaking bed's protest to their activity.

Noble asked Sudan where he came from as they repaired the roof on the store.

"Alabama. Mister Lincoln, he set us free but he done forgot we had to eat. See, the master always fed us. I just supposed folks would feed us. My, my, I missed a lot of meals coming here."

"We appreciate all you do."

"I'm glad. But Noble, you ever get low on money, you don't have to pay me 'cause I like being here, like them Osages do. You and the Misses are good folks."

Finished with the chore, Noble started off the roof. Spotted Horse came riding in, searching around and when he saw him, the Osage rode directly up to him.

"What's going on?"

"Wichitas want to winter here. Chief Tall Timber promises no whiskey this time."

"Tell them to come in peace."

The Osage nodded and trotted off to carry word back to the Indians.

"Who are the Wichitas?" Sudan asked.

"An Indian tribe that wintered here last year. An outlaw sold them some bad whiskey, they got drunk, scared Fleta and the Osage women. But I think they've learned their lesson."

Noble's thoughts went to Izer Goodman. That rotten devil was probably down in the Territory stirring up trouble. One day, Noble vowed, he would settle the score with Izer Goodman for all the trouble he caused.

A week later, two men arrived driving a wagon and two jaded draft horses.

"We'll trade you the wagon and horses for two saddles and fresh horse," the sharp nosed younger man offered.

Noble walked around the rig examining it. The wagon was a well-kept farm vehicle, hardly the property of the two scruffy looking men.

"Mister—?" Noble asked, recalling the men had not offered their names.

"Thomas," the sharper nosed man said reluctantly. "William Thomas."

"I'll have to send for the horses; they're out grazing." Noble studied the gaunt sorrel team. They were well-bred Belgian mares.

Sudan beckoned Noble over to the side. "You going to trade for them?"

"I guess," Noble said, keeping a cautious eye on the two men.

"Those mares would sure have powerful mule colts," Sudan informed him. "Yes, sir, mated to a big jack, they'd have mules that could pull two wagons at once."

"Sudan, find two old saddles. Then have Spotted Horse bring in two Indian ponies. This pair ain't telling the truth. I figure they stole this outfit. They've nearly run the mares to death getting here. As much as I hate to trade for stolen goods, I'd hate to see those good draft horses ruined."

"Those two sure bear watching," Sudan agreed.

Noble crossed back to the pair. "I'll trade with you. The horses will be here in a little while."

Thomas nodded. His partner seemed nervous and edgy. "How long?"

"About an hour," Noble said.

"You sell whiskey?"

"No, we don't sell it here."

When Spotted Horse brought in the two ponies, if Thomas and his companion were not pleased, they gave no indication. They saddled up, each took a sack of things from the wagon and left at a stiff trot. Noble was relieved to see them go. Even the Osages armed themselves and sat nearby to keep an eye on them.

Sudan's eyes held an eagerness as he strode over to unhitch the mares. Noble helped him undo the harness, smiling at the black man's soothing words that he spoke to the team.

Fleta and the Osage women waited to see what else was in the wagon. Noble climbed over the front wheel and Spotted Horse came in over the back tailgate under the canvas hoop.

Noble spotted the woman's underclothing. When he picked them he noticed they were torn and bloodstained. Quickly he rolled them up and hid them. A few other signs suggested a violent struggle took place in the wagon. He was sickened when he realized what must have happened to the owners of the rig. His jaw tightened with anger.

When Noble emerged from the wagon, Fleta immediately noticed his troubled expression. "What's wrong, Noble?"

"Spotted Horse and I will unload the wagon," he said curtly.

His tone told her enough. She herded the Osage women and children back inside the store. She knew Noble would tell her later what he found in the wagon. In the distance, she heard Luke shout at Noble. "Is there someone dead in there?"

"No, Luke, but you better go to the house."

"Thank God," Fleta murmured softly. But she had a sick feeling when she recalled the look on Noble's face.

Chapter Eight

On their way back from Independence, Toby Evans and a few of his cowboys stopped at Noble's Fort. Evans produced a pocket worn letter from Cedric Patterson for Noble. The missive was urgent, but since the drover had carried it across Nebraska and Kansas, the envelope was creased, dirty, and unfortunately, over sixty days old.

The message from the Patterson's urged Noble to return to Independence and see a certain lawyer. The possibility of purchasing the land around the fort looked very promising and he needed to accept or reject the offer.

Noble became concerned he might be too late to buy the property since so much time had elapsed.

"The Wichita's won't get drunk this time," he assured Fleta as he prepared to leave for Missouri. "I have Chief Tall Timber's word. Sudan can handle anything that Barge and River can't. I told Spotted Horse that I would take him with me. We'll ride hard and won't be gone more than a week."

Fleta reluctantly agreed. The land title needed to be settled; she had no wish to be ousted from her new house, especially since things were going so well. Sudan had promised to add on a couple of rooms to the back of the store. He was going down in the Indian Territory with the oxen to bring back enough logs to make a real house behind the store. Fleta looked forward to sleeping away from the smelly dry goods.

Noble noticed Spotted Horse chose a pair of waist overalls from the store. For the trip, Mannah hand sewed him a red shirt and a new fringed buckskin coat adorned with bead work. Noble was secretly amused at the Indian's actions. Obviously Spotted Horse had no intentions of allowing the people of Independence to think he was some poor, blanket-ass Indian.

The Osage's saddle had a blanket cover, and the Colt rifle stuck out of a saddle boot. All this was mounted on a leggy Kentucky horse that Noble traded for. He had to admit the Indian looked prosperous. Even the eagle feathers in his braids fluttered with newness.

Fleta had written three letters for Noble to post. She found addresses in the wagon Noble suspected as stolen. The wagon owners' name was Thomas. Surmising that the letters in the wagon to be from relatives, Noble urged Fleta to write, telling them about the fate of their kin. At Noble's insistence, she wrote that they had found the wagon empty and suspected foul play. It was a bleak Christian duty Fleta performed and she was profoundly relieved when she finished the missives.

"Don't fidget so much, Noble," she said as she cut his shoulder-length sandy hair. "I swear you act like you're nervous. But you'd look like some sort of ruffian going to Independence without a hair cut."

"You're right, but that doesn't mean I enjoy getting one," he retorted with a mocking smile.

"Sit still." Fleta shook her head. Noble could certainly get worked up and impatient when he had something to do.

"Fleta," Noble's voice was grim, "I sure hate leaving you alone, but I don't have much choice. This land thing has to be settled."

"Noble, hold still or you're going to have a big bald spot," she scolded, inwardly hiding her sadness at the thought of him being away so long. "You've spent all day telling me how safe we are. Now you're worried. Well, I'm not, so just sit still," she finished with more confidence than she felt.

"Yes, ma'am."

The ride on horseback only required three days. The weather

was dreary, chilly, and uneventful. Noble was sore from sleeping on the ground and grimaced at his stiff joints when he dismounted in Independence.

Patterson's Store looked familiar and welcome. Noble unbuttoned his long canvas coat and stood watching Spotted Horse's face. Despite its blandness, he knew the Osage carefully observed the facets of civilization.

Spotted Horse dismounted and looked around. "This is where the squaw peed?" he asked with a grin.

Noble smiled dryly. "I believe there were more wagons in the street then. The pack horses were lined up to that corner." He gestured with his thumb. Spotted Horse shook his head with amused laughter, then followed Noble into the store.

"Mr. McCurtain!" Alex called warmly. "We wondered if you were having problems. We've been expecting you for some time."

"No," Noble said, shaking the man's hand. "No problem. The letter was late getting to me. We rode here as fast as we could after receiving it."

"Alex, I'd like you to meet Chief Spotted Horse."

The store keeper inclined his head slightly in greeting. "Nice to meet you, Chief." Spotted Horse nodded his acknowledgement.

Alex ushered them to the office in the rear of the store.

"Am I too late to make an offer on the property?" Noble asked anxiously.

"No." Alex shook his head then cleared his throat. "Father," he addressed Cedric who was sitting at his desk engrossed in looking at invoices. "This is Chief Spotted Horse, a friend of Noble's."

The elder man stood up and removed his reading glasses, He smiled broadly. "Glad to meet you Chief. Nice to see you again, Noble."

"Good store here," the Osage said in a voice of authority that Noble couldn't recall him using before. My Lord, Noble mused, give him a title and he's a regular ambassador.

"Tell Noble about the land, Father," Alex urged.

"Ah, yes. The Southern Kansas Railroad owns the property that your store is situated on. Congress awarded them that land. They will keep a right of way east and west, but they need the money badly.''

"How badly?''

"Well, they weren't certain just where your store is situated on their property, but you can buy six thousand acres for one-thousand dollars.'' The elder Patterson waved his finger like a gun. "And you will have a federal guaranteed deed to your place. A fort isn't it?''

"Yes.'' Noble wanted to shout for joy at the news. Instead he clenched his teeth and paced around the room viewing the floor. He could hardly believe it was true—clear title to the land.

"That is good news, isn't it?'' Cedric asked, frowning at Noble's preoccupied look.

"Hell, yes,'' Noble lifted his head and grinned. "It's the best damned news I've heard in my life. Let's go get it done.''

"Tomorrow,'' the senior Patterson said. "The lawyer is up at the fort on army business. Nice man, Albert Wooten, someday he'll be governor.''

"I'll vote for him,'' Noble said vehemently.

"Come on, look at the new Colts we just got in,'' Alex invited.

"Yeah.'' Noble motioned for the unimpressed Osage to follow them. "Toby Evans showed me his new model.''

"They're .44's with side ejection. They'll outshoot anything,'' Alex explained as they went to the guncase. "The grips are larger. Samuel Colt did himself proud. I even have the short-barreled sheriff's model.'' He handed a new and well-oiled weapon to Noble.

Noble spun the cylinder and tried the ejector. He balanced both models in his hand. "I like the longer barrel,'' he decided. A smile spread across his face at the double holster set that Alex spread on the counter. Noble raised a brow when he noticed the holster even had loops for the rim fire ammunition.

Noble watched the Osage getting the feel of a lever action rifle. "Is that the Henry rifle?''

"No. A Winchester .44/40 and it's the rifle for the plains. That model has a cartridge that will reach out. No fizzling short shells. The lever action is improved. It has all steel working parts.''

Spotted Horse smiled privately at Noble when he handed him the oily-smelling weapon.

"Do they work good?" Noble asked.

"Sure do. We can hardly keep them in stock. They're very popular."

"I'll need four for my people at the fort." Noble looked questioningly at the Osage. The Indian nodded.

"No," he said, turning back to Alex. "Make that five, just in case we have trouble."

"Do you expect to have trouble?" Alex asked, alarmed.

"No," Noble said, his mind for a moment on Izer Goodman. "But we have had some and could have more. We'll get those guns and ammunition tomorrow."

"Noble?" Alex's brow was lined with worry. "You better leave your other pistols here. The marshal has a gun law on the streets."

Noble shrugged. "You sure are getting civilized around here."

"I know how you frontier people must feel, but we're trying to make this town safe and respectable."

"Well, thanks for the warning." Noble laid the pair of .36's from his waistband on the counter. He hitched up his pants, feeling almost undressed without the guns in his belt.

"The Reagan Hotel is a clean place to stay and the food's not bad. It's two blocks down the street." Alex pointed to the left.

"Thanks. We'll go put our horses up."

After stabling their mounts, the two men went to the hotel. The desk clerk eyed Spotted Horse dubiously.

"I must warn you there is no cooking in the room," the haughty little man said, turning the book around to read Noble's signature. "Noble...McCurtain and Spotted Horse."

The man blinked and took a slight step backward. "Well, Mister McCurtain, we have had problems with aborigines building fires in their room," he explained, wrinkling his nose in distaste.

"He's an Osage," Noble stated curtly.

"Osage, whatever. He is still an aborigine."

Noble looked at the man contemptuously. "Come on Chief, this man is obviously an idiot. He may even get scalped if he continues to call every tribe by that stupid name. We don't want to spoil our dinners by witnessing such a bloody sight, huh?" Noble gave the man a pitying look, satisfied by his pale complexion that the mention of scalping had had its effect. He turned and with the room key safely in his hands, moved toward the restaurant.

When the waiter came to their table, he gave them a skeptical look. Irritated by the lack of respect they were receiving, Noble looked the man squarely in the eye.

"This is a Chief. He's killed a hundred Cheyenne."

The man's eyes widened with fear. His adam's apple bobbed up and down. "Y—yes sir."

After the waiter went through a long list of meals like squab and others, Noble ordered the roast pork, deciding the fancy dressed people seated around them could eat that other stuff.

Spotted Horse sneezed when he sniffed the pepper. The action drew a dozen stares. Sometimes while he ate, the Indian used his knife rather than his fork. All in all, Noble was proud of him.

"They collect money after you eat," Noble explained.

Spotted Horse shook his head. "What if you do not pay? Do they squeeze the food out of you?" The Chief leaned across the table. "Him believe I killed plenty Cheyenne?"

"I think so." Noble was amused at the Indian's logic. Not much passed the chief. Ready to go to their room, Noble thought they had drawn enough impertinent stares for one day.

"Come on, let's go build a fire in the room," he said.

"Have a wild party like the Wichitas," Spotted Horse said, stern-faced as stone.

"Yes, that's what we should do." Noble unlocked the room door. Once inside, the Osage sat on the floor, obviously disdaining the beds and wooden chairs.

A sharp rap on the door drew Noble up from the bed. For a moment he wished he had his pistols. He nodded reassuringly at the sight of Spotted Horse's knife.

"Who's there?"

"Captain Rourke, U S Army," came the clipped reply.

"All right." Noble went toward the door, wondering what the man wanted.

"Mr. McCurtain?" The man was gray at the temples, ramrod tall with a weathered face.

"Yes."

"I understand that you have a plains chief here with you. I wonder if I might have the courtesy of asking him a few questions."

Noble opened the door for the man. Rourke swept on his gold braid, decorated felt hat and his boot heels clicked when he stepped into the room.

"Have a chair, Captain," Noble offered. "The chief does not care for them."

"Thank you." Rourke sat down. "Good day, sir," the officer spoke to Spotted Horse, who remained seated on the floor. At least Noble noted the man did not offer to shake the chief's hand. Indians thought the custom very funny. He had seen Barge and Rivers shaking hands in private and laughing about the white man's silly ritual; Spotted Horse was accustomed to doing so with many settlers passing through the fort.

"He understands English," Noble assured Rourke.

"Chief, what are the conditions in southern Kansas now?"

Spotted Horse looked quickly at Noble.

"He means is there peace there?" Noble interpreted the question.

The Osage nodded. Then he began using a halted English that almost made Noble laugh. "Plenty peace. Plenty buffalo. Be good winter."

"Thank God," the man offered piously. He turned to Noble. "Did he say all the tribes in your region are peaceful?"

Noble nodded. "Spotted Horse, I think he wants to know if you expect any fighting?"

"No fighting."

"That's good news. We have reports that the Sioux, Cheyenne and the Pawnees are all in an uproar. We don't have enough troops to contain them."

"Rest easy. Things are peaceful with the Osage and the Wichitas," Noble said.

"Mr. McCurtain, the military knows about your good works. Your temperance actions are needed all over the frontier. Whiskey seems to fire up these people to atrocities beyond belief.

"Why just a year ago, not three days ride south of here, a man was found who had been horribly scalped and mutilated."

Red Barber, Noble decided, though he didn't ask the officer the man's name.

The captain rose and gave the Osage a sharp salute. "The army is grateful. Chief Spotted Horse. And to you too, Mr. McCurtain. We are at your service if you need us."

"If I ever need help, I'll sure send word." Noble rose to open the door for the man.

Noble listened for the officer's retreating foot steps. He turned to the Osage. "By damn, Spotted Horse, we are now in with the army." They both laughed at the irony.

"You plenty big chief here."

Spotted Horse grunted solemnly and they both laughed again.

As Noble lay in bed, he thought of all the things he had to tell Fleta when he got home. She would laugh at Spotted Horse's peace-keeping role. Even Red Barber's demise had become an Indian atrocity. The army's notion about the plains Indians was incomplete for people who were supposed to be protecting the frontier. Noble looked up at the ceiling. He ached to be home; this was not his place.

Before dawn, the lumpy bed hurt his back. Noble awoke and lighted the lamp. He knew the Osage was awake.

"Plenty noise in white man's village all night," the Chief complained.

Noble agreed. "Let's go look for a pack horse to carry our new rifles home and get some trinkets for everyone. We might find a big mare for Sudan's mule project."

They ate breakfast in a narrow cafe then in the gray dawn walked to the livery stable. Noble felt undressed without his pistols.

"I need a mare with draft blood," Noble told the sleepy eyed, bowler hatted man who led them down through the sour smelling stables.

"Horses are high, Mr. McCurtain. The army needs hundreds. Are there any good ones in your part of the country?"

"How much do you pay for them, Mr.—" Noble asked curiously, a half-formed plan beginning in his mind.

"Doone's the name. Twenty bucks a head."

Noble knew the man would pay more, but now he was interested in buying one.

"There she be," the man pointed in the lot.

Noble climbed the fence. She was a blood bay with feathered feet. Her trot and carriage distinguished her from the other saddle stock in the pen.

With his arm hooked over the top pole, Noble watched her high stepping action. Sudan would like her. Noble stepped back off the fence and started for the barn.

"Well what do you think?" Doone asked, hurrying to catch up with them.

"How much?"

"Which one?"

Noble sighed impatiently. "The one you brought me back to look at."

The man shook his head. "Damn, at six thirty in the morning, you're hard to trade with. Fifty dollars."

"Twenty-five."

"No way! The army will pay me forty for her."

Noble was silent for a moment. "I'll bring you three horses in the spring and take her now."

"She's worth cash-now."

Noble shrugged, striving to appear indifferent. "Come on, Spotted Horse."

"Wait," Doone surrendered. "You could get killed and scalped and I would be out the cost of her."

"That's the gamble you'll have to take," Noble said, turning to face the man.

"I've heard lots about you McCurtain. Can you bring me several horses next spring?"

Noble didn't answer immediately. Finally he drawled slowly, "Well, that depends. I will send you three sound horses for her. If we capture or trade for any more, I'll send them." He turned to the Osage. "Go get Sudan's new mare."

"Does that chief work for you?" Doone asked, a little taken aback by the notion.

"We're partners," Noble corrected him. "He takes care of the Indian deals, I take care of the white men ones."

Doone looked after the Osage who had grabbed a rope and set out down the stables at a trot.

"I'd say you had a real good thing going on out there these days."

Noble smiled with cynicism. People like Doone were really frightened about the frontier. Either that, or he was isolated from the truth.

A while later, he and Spotted Horse waited for Patterson's to open up. Their three horses were tied to the hitch rail. The chief squatted on the porch and Noble leaned against a porch post, watching the early morning traffic. Dray wagons and the open freighters passed by. Briefly Noble wondered where his ex-boss, Ben Rutherford, was at that moment.

"Noble!" Spotted Horse spoke sharply.

Noble looked up to see Izer Goodman riding out of the alley across the street. His pistol was aimed at Noble.

"Die, McCurtain, you no good son of a bitch!" Izer shouted.

Noble dove off the porch just before a spray of bullets shattered the glass front of the store. Crouched by the legs of his horses, he cursed his unarmed state. More shots zinged. The gray horse screamed then tore loose from the rail.

"That no-good-bastard has shot my horse!" Noble raged as he rose to his feet. The Osage had lunged for the Colt rifle sticking out of his saddle boot.

"Give me the gun!" Noble shouted as he watched the two retreating figures dressed in buckskin, riding pell mell out of range down the street.

"Damnit! That was Izer Goodman and Tennessee Dawson," Noble fumed, pounding the hitch rail with his right hand.

He walked around to where the gray horse floundered on the ground. A bloody froth bubbled from the horse's mouth. Noble was sickened as the gallant horse tried to rise. Those bastards would pay for this.

A deputy waving a pistol, came hurrying forward.

"Give me your gun," Noble ordered the man.

"What the hell for?"

Noble reached for the chief's Colt rifle, then aimed it at the gray's forehead. A blast of the gun and the animal succumbed to death, out of his misery. Noble stood trembling in anger. He never noticed when Spotted Horse took the gun back.

"You again!" a swaggering voice said in disgust. The chief marshal stepped forward. "Every time you come here we have trouble."

"You'll have a damn sight more if I get those two in my gun sights."

"What two?"

"The pair that rode out of that alley and commenced shooting at us." Noble pointed to the alley. "Your stupid gun law nearly got me and this chief of the Osage gunned down."

"By who?"

"Izer Goodman and Tennessee Dawson. They're killers, road agents, and they trade whiskey to the Indians."

"Can you prove all that?" the marshal asked.

"I won't have to. Next time I'll kill him myself," Noble said.

"Well, I hope to God, it ain't in Independence."

"Are you all right, Mr. McCurtain?" Noble turned and saw Captain Rourke dismounting.

"Marshal, Mr. McCurtain's work is too important for him to be shot down by some local bandits. His work in his region could save hundreds of civilian lives."

Noble almost laughed at the berating the military man gave the lawman. Rourke was damn serious about this Indian business.

"My superiors would like you and the chief to come to the post to meet them."

"Sorry, Captain." Noble tried to be as diplomatic as he could. "I have some business to complete here in town. My wife is home practically alone. We have a long ride ahead of us and I've lost the best damn horse I ever owned." He cast a regretful look at the silent gray.

"Please allow the military to replace the horse. I'll send for one at once. Your service is very important to the army."

"That won't be necessary—"

"I insist," Rourke interrupted him. "Within the hour, you shall have a horse."

"Thank you then." He motioned for the chief to go ahead of him inside the store.

Inside, Noble tried to apologize for the shattered glass, but the Pattersons seemed unconcerned about the damage.

"I'm sorry, Noble," Alex said, with a rueful shake of his head. "If you had had your pistols, this would never have happened."

Noble waved away his apology. His mind was still preoccupied with the captain's words about his work with the Indians. Perhaps this peace business was more serious than he originally thought. Maybe there was more to it than he realized. Rourke certainly seemed eager to give him any assistance.

"Don't worry about it, Alex," he said, but Alex continued to apologize for the shooting. "We may have hit innocent people if we'd had our guns."

"What will you ride home?" Alex asked as Noble loaded the brass ammunition in the new .44 side arms.

"The army says they will supply me a horse. If not, I'll buy one from Doone."

Cedric Patterson returned from supervising the clean up in the front. "A very terrible incident," he apologized. "We're so glad that you are all right." Then the senior Patterson looked very seriously at him. "Noble, do you need any money to close this land deal?"

"No, thank you. We've had a good year," Noble told him, pleased that his supplier obviously considered him worthy of a loan.

Noble slid the new pistols in the holsters, then buckled them on. They were heavy, but had twice the fire power of his old cap and balls. To hell with the gun law. He planned to leave as soon as the land deal was closed.

He found the attorney's office. The lawyer Wooten was a well dressed man with mutton chop sideburns. He looked shocked by the gold coins that Noble stacked on his desk.

"Highly unusual," the lawyer commented, "but perfectly good money, of course. You'll need to sign here." He pointed to a space on the parchment page. "Then after filing, the land will be yours."

Noble bent over and paused. One stroke of the pen and 50 twenty-dollar gold pieces would change him from landless to landed. His uncle, who owned forty acres, would be shocked if he knew about the deal. Why, the man could plow for a week and not even get to the other side of Noble's land.

"Is something wrong, sir?" Wooten asked.

"No, just thinking." He re-dipped the pen and scrawled his name. His signature reminded him he still needed to post Fleta's letters to the Thomas family. She would be terribly upset if he didn't send them after all the pains that she had taken to write them.

"There is the matter of the recording and my fee," Wooten said as Noble rose to his feet.

"How much?"

"Forty dollars, sir."

"That seems fair enough." Noble dug the coins out of his pocket and put them on the desk. He sighed inwardly, hoping to get out of town before he spent any more money.

He left Wooten's office and went to post Fleta's letters. He just came out of the post office onto the wooden sidewalk when someone called his name. His right hand shot for the butt of his new Colt.

"Mr. McCurtain!" Captain Rourke and two non-coms rode through the traffic toward him. Noble blinked his eyes at the horse they led. It was a gray. A larger horse perhaps by a hand than his dead one. And a stallion to boot.

"Here is your horse," Rourke said, his face flushed from his quick trip.

Noble stepped out in the street to inspect the animal.

"My commander, Colonel George Armstrong Custer, sent him along with his compliments."

"Well." Noble breathed through his lips, overwhelmed by the man's generosity. "He's much too fine a horse just for me."

"No, sir. The commander wanted you to have him."

"Well, you tell Colonel Custer that he's much too generous and that I'm obliged to him." Noble took the lead and let the horse circle around him. Traffic stopped and people gawked at the tall-hatted frontiersman and his fancy stallion.

"What do you think, Chief?"

Spotted Horse looked about to bust out of his fringed clothing. "He's a gawd damn good one, Noble."

"Yeah," A halted freighter shouted. "And I hate Injuns, but he's right about the silver horse."

Noble ducked his head. Enough of being the spectacle, he thought with a grin. He swung aboard his new mount and set out in a run. George Custer, huh? Well, he'd meet him some day and thank the man personally for such a generous gift.

Fleta, he said silently, you aren't going to believe all the stories I have to tell. I lost one horse and now have a better one. Fleta, I'm coming home on a helluva horse.

Chapter Nine

Fleta watched for Noble, knowing he would be returning soon. From her vantage point outside the gate, she could scan the entire brown prairie. A cold wind swept her dress around her legs.

She missed the trees of Arkansas. From her childhood in Tennessee to her life in Arkansas, there had always been trees. Trees to chop for firewood, to saw for lumber, and for shade. It was hard to adjust to the Kansas prairie where trees were scarce. She had a fleeting notion of joining Sudan to see the trees that he planned to cut down deep in the Indian Territory. The only trees nearby were a few spindly ones south on the creek that served the Indians as a communal bathing place. The hills at home would be bare now except for the dark cedars and a few pines. She wondered if Wilbourne would be there to see them. Wilbourne. Strange she had not thought of him in a long time. Perhaps because she had been so busy with the store or perhaps it was because Noble was gone. Her thoughts were divided between the two men; niggling doubts inside left her queasy. The man she had abandoned would no doubt survive. Oh, why didn't Noble come home?

She turned and walked through the gate. Sudan appeared, startling her. He was a giant figure in his buffalo coat, his wiry hair bushy and in need of a cut.

"He'll be coming back soon, Misses," Sudan said quietly.

Fleta smiled at him. "Yes, I know. Guess I'm just a worrier, Sudan."

He nodded. "Noble McCurtain is a powerful man for his years. But I guess you knowed all that when you married him."

Fleta swallowed a painful lump. She wasn't really married to Noble. She lowered her head to hide the sudden ache of tears.

"Misses Fleta, I never meant no harm," Sudan said, horrified at seeing her sad expression.

"I know, I know." The wind stung her face as she looked up at the gentle man. "It's a long story, Sudan. Yes, my husband is a good man," she said, emphasizing the word husband.

The black man smiled with understanding. My woman, he thought, is buried in a grove of maples at home. 'Cept my home is here now, 'cause I'd probably cry every day if I had to look at her cemetery plot.

Sudan studied the eastern horizon. Noble, he thought silently, you come home real soon. I ache to go down south in the Indian Territory and get some logs for the Misses' new rooms. Rivers said there were some big trees there. Walnuts with rich brown heartwood would last a lifetime. Luke probably would use them when the property was passed to him. Sudan knew Luke was not Noble's true son, but the boy came from good stock. Maybe that was what was bothering the Misses. She must have lost Luke's daddy.

Sudan walked back to his blacksmith shop. The edge of his hewing axe was razor sharp when he tested it with his thumb. All the yokes were in good shape. He had checked and replaced all the bad links on the chains. Now he was bored. He sighed heavily. Noble McCurtain, you hurry that gray horse on home now.

Noble was pushed harder to get home. The new stallion was a handful and the miles had not settled him. Spotted Horse's mount kept up but Noble was concerned that they might be pushing the good Kentucky horse too hard. Indians had little regard for a horse, except to use them for their own purposes.

"Let's go on to the fort tonight," Noble said as they rested and chewed on buffalo jerky.

"It will be after sundown when we get there," Spotted Horse said.

Noble twisted off another bite and shrugged. Sundown was soon enough; he was anxious to tell Fleta about the land purchase, the stallion, and Izer's attempt to shoot him. Maybe he wouldn't tell her about Izer. But no, that wasn't right. She'd have to know. There would never be any peace until Izer Goodman was dead.

He swung up in the saddle. Colonel Custer had been generous. Maybe someday he could send him a suitable colt from the horse to repay him.

The next morning, Sudan ducked to enter the store. The sight of Noble seated at the table pleased him. He heard him arrive during the night, but knowing Noble would be too tired to do any talking, he waited until morning to visit him. The stallion in the pen outside was a new arrival. Where was the gray horse that Noble thought so much of?

"Sudan, hello there. Come and have a seat," Noble invited. "Fleta says you're eager to go cut the logs for her house."

"Yes sir, Mr. Noble." He sat down opposite Noble, glad to have his boss home again. Now the Misses would be happy.

"Well, I brought home some new repeaters and ammunition," Noble said, sipping coffee. "You take one in case you need it. Is Rivers going with you?"

"Yes sir." He watched Noble rise and collect a new lever action rifle. He took the gun eagerly from Noble's outstretched hand. "This is a fine gun."

Sudan handled the gun almost lovingly. So this was a Winchester, he mused. Why, a man could stop an army with a gun like this. Now that was Noble McCurtain, always giving you something. He'd give a black man a new gun and send him off with a fortune in tools and draft animals without a second thought. Why, if I was a mind to, I could go to parts unknown with it all. Trust, that's what Noble McCurtain had, and respect for old Sudan. His chest swelled with pride and he beamed a wide toothy smile at his benefactor.

Sudan was glad that Rivers came along with him to cut the logs. He could see Rivers was proud of the new gun. That Osage had a curiosity about blacksmith work. Indians were different. They'd watch and watch, then one day they would do whatever they had been observing.

Besides, Rivers drove oxen better than the other Indians. Some of his words were probably curses in his own language, but Sudan enjoyed listening to the Indian swear at the dull oxen.

He and Rivers left at mid-morning. A bright sun promised to warm them. Six sets of oxen and the Belgium mares, now shiny and spirited, left the fort with Sudan who rode proudly on his big high-stepping, new mare.

They made camp before sundown. Rivers said the timber was still two days south. Sudan struck steel to flint and made a fire to cook the beans that Fleta had sent along.

"You sleep," Rivers said, "I'll guard."

"I'll help you. You come and wake me for the last half of the night."

Rivers never mentioned an enemy being nearby. Perhaps the Osage was just concerned that someone might steal the stock. Sudan puffed on his stub of a pipe. The smoke he drew tasted dry and sweet. The temperature was dropping. He would sleep until Rivers woke him.

Two days passed uneventfully. They drove into a river bottom forested with impressive black-trunked walnuts.

The steers were turned out to graze the brown grass. After hobbling the horses to keep them nearby, the men set a buffalo hide cover over a frame of willows to use for a shelter and to cache their supplies.

Sudan began chopping the first tree. The wedged chips flew. He felt his muscles flex. He enjoyed this almost as much as making love to a willing women. Chip by chip, his axe bit out the wood. This work was as important as smithing.

Rivers limbed the fallen trees. Then he watched Sudan hew out the square logs from the rounded trunks.

On Sunday, Sudan rested. His muscles were sore but he was satisfied that in a few days he would have all the wood they could sled home with the oxen. Rivers used the sabbath to sleep.

Taking his rifle, Sudan roamed the bottoms. They had adequate camp meat from the deer he had shot earlier. As he walked the river's edge, an odd object on the far bank caught his eye. A body lay on the erosion-exposed shore across the river. The person was either dead or unconscious for no one slept in such a place or in such an unnatural position.

Sudan removed his boots. He slid off his leather pants and placed them over his new rifle to hide it. Soon he was waist deep in chilly water, his bare feet on the smooth rocks and soft mud. His brown eyes held fast on the figure across the river.

The cold air struck his wet skin as he waded out of the shallows. When he was near enough to get a good look at the body, he was surprised to see it was a woman. An Indian woman. Cautiously he searched around to be sure no one else was nearby. The side of her head was mud smeared from where she had fallen or fainted. He rolled her over and whistled softly. She was perhaps twenty years old; a nasty looking wound oozed from her right shoulder. She'd been shot.

He gave a quick check of the bank above. Nothing. The woman was alive and moaning weakly. Her buckskin blouse was blood soaked over her breast. Sudan had many questions he wanted to ask her. The pressing question was, how close were her enemies? He scooped her up and plunged into the chilly river. He felt an urgency to get back to his weapon.

Though her limp weight was no burden, Sudan remained concerned that he might slip and douse his new found obligation. He ignored the icy cold water. Past the deepest swirling water, he held her high and turned slightly. Had he heard horses? He strained to listen. Nothing but crows calling.

Gently he laid her down on the grass, then pulled on his britches, and boots. No time to dry; he had to get back and wake up Rivers.

The woman obviously needed medical attention. Her face was beautiful, but pale. Her wound was seeping again. Sudan frowned and scanned the far bank. He could hear nothing except the river's rushing. He laid the rifle across the woman, scooped her up again and hurried back to camp. His urgency was a mixture of concern for the woman and the fear of whoever might be after her.

He glanced down at her face again. Her skin was olive, although pale due to a loss of blood. Her nose was slender and her lashes dark and very long.

Sudan was relieved when Rivers emerged from the shelter at his approach.

"Get some water," he instructed the Osage. "She's been shot."

Carefully Sudan placed her inside on his bedroll, laying the rifle nearby. He drew the Bowie knife from his belt, then gently split open the pull-over leather blouse to expose the wound above her breast.

Her eyes opened and fear immediately flashed across them.

"I am a friend," Sudan said quietly. The words did not satisfy her and she tried to rise. Sudan put the knife aside to physically restrain her from getting up.

"Hold still. My name's Sudan. I ain't going to kill you, but if you keep fighting me, the bleeding's gonna kill you for sure."

Her dark brown eyes glazed over and she fell into unconsciousness. Sudan scowled, afraid that she might be dying.

"Lordy, don't do that, girl. Hold on, Injun. We can fix that hole. You just don't go and die on me." He reached for his saddle bag and drew out a cotton sack that would serve as a bandage.

Where in the hell was Rivers? Damn, he was taking long enough to get water.

The Osage threw open the flap of the shelter. Something was wrong. Sudan could see it in his face.

"Riders coming." Rivers set the bucket down and gestured with his thumb over his shoulder.

"How many?"

The Osage indicated several. Sudan jerked up his lever action and headed out, rising to his full height once he was outside. He levered a shell in the chamber and viewed the invaders. River did the same with his rifle.

Short of the clearing, a buck wearing a soldier's cap raised his hand in a peace sign.

"What the hell does he want, Rivers?"

"They're Wichitas. Not ones who come to fort."

"Ask him what he wants," Sudan said, noticing the war paint on the five men's faces.

The Osage said something that Sudan could not understand. Sudan quickly appraised the enemy. They were riding war horses. Two of them carried lances and buffalo shields. The muzzle loaders the others carried did not look impressive. Their leader had two plow handles sticking out of his waistband. Probably cap and ball pistols and the only weapons capable of rapid fire.

Rivers' exchange with the leader was brief. The Wichita chief was angry.

"What does he say?" Sudan hissed, growing impatient with the scowling bunch. They didn't wear robes, despite the cold; so obviously the Indians were prepared to fight.

"He says the woman is Comanche and belongs to him. She threatened his life, so he must kill her."

"He aims to kill her, huh?"

Rivers nodded without hesitation.

Sudan glared at them. "Tell him no!"

The Osage seemed undecided. Sudan drew a deep breath and raised up his rifle barrel. His wet britches were cold and the leather had begun to stiffen. He hoped he could move fast enough if he had to.

"Tell him *no!*" he repeated.

The Wichita spoke and Rivers quickly interpreted. "He says to tell Beaver Tail what the black man wants."

"The woman," Sudan said curtly.

At his brief words, Beaver Tail laughed mockingly and the other bucks joined him.

Sudan clamped his teeth in rage. So the son-of-a-bitch understood English. Well, fine. That would make it easier to deal with the red devil.

"Beaver Tail!" Sudan shouted. "You go for one of those pistols, get yourself ready to die. Rivers and me got those repeaters loaded to the top."

If the Chief understood Sudan's threat, his cold silence at least betrayed that he was considering the Winchesters.

"Move a ways over there," Sudan said under his breath to Rivers. "These dumb asses are itching to die."

The Osage obeyed, his rifle at the ready. Beaver Tail was forced to dart his eyes from one to the other of them.

"Beaver Tail, either drive or cut!" Sudan ordered, suppressing a cold shiver. "Do it now or git!"

For a moment, Sudan suspected the man was tempted to jerk

one of his pistols out of the blue waistband. Then he spoke to his braves.

Sudan's finger was on the trigger, ready to fire.

The chief turned his horse around as if to leave and with his back turned made the move Sudan expected. The chief went for one of his pistols.

Sudan's Winchester barked and the leader pitched forward over the neck of his pony. Rivers took the lead lance-bearer off his horse. Powder smoke boiled as Sudan moved to his right, aiming the .44/.40 with deadly accuracy.

Men wailed and the battle was over in a matter of minutes.

Six Indians, as well as three horses, lay dead or wounded. Rivers rose from his knees and nodded at Sudan.

The rifles were everything he expected them to be. He nodded his approval when Rivers mentioned he would check the dead. Sudan went back inside the shelter and dropped to his knees beside the injured women. A single shot rang out. Sudan cocked his head. Either one of the wounded was now dead or a horse had been put out of its misery.

With the kerchief, Sudan washed the blood on the woman's shoulder and the top of her firm breast. When he rinsed the cloth, a crimson stain spread in the water.

Grimly, he studied the wound. The bullet was still in her shoulder. It probably came from one of Beaver Tail's pistols, Sudan surmised. He measured the size of the hole with his small finger. He recalled in their camp supplies was a small knife. He drew it out and tested the edge. Sudan knew he would need a stone to whet it on.

When he drew the flap back, he saw Rivers scalping the Wichitas. Sweet Jesus, help me. He turned away, so shaken by the scene he gave up his search for a rock to use as a whetstone.

Once again, Sudan knelt over his patient, then began to prove with the knife blade. The blood flowed freely again. The woman twisted in pain. He used his palm on her breastbone to restrain her when he gouged for the lead with the blade. The knife's point tipped the bullet and he felt it loosen.

"Lie still, Comanche girl. I have it. It's coming out. I've about got the dammed ball out of you," Sudan grunted through panted breaths.

Her eyes flickered and blinked as Sudan held the bullet between his bloodied finger tips.

"I got it. See. Lord, gal, you'll be getting better in no time," he promised as he washed off the fresh blood and pressed a bandage against the wound.

"Wish I knew how to stop your bleeding," he spoke his thoughts aloud. "There's a woman back home who saved black spider webs for this sort of thing. I wish she was here." Sudan shook his head. "I know how to stop this, but damn, it sure will hurt bad."

There seemed nothing else to do but what he had to do.

"Rivers! Bring me one of their gunpowder horns and hurry up about it," he shouted.

The Osage came inside carrying the powder horn.

"Hold her down," Sudan ordered as he poured the gray-black granules out of the polished white cow horn and onto the wound.

"I'm going out and get some fire. You hold her good," Sudan said.

He pushed out of the shelter and lighted a twig from the fire's coals. Shielding the flame, he carefully backed up inside the lean-to. Taking a deep breath, Sudan straddled the woman's hips.

"Put something in her mouth to bite down on," he told the Osage.

Rivers hesitated, then after a brief struggle, stuck a rein from a bridle in her mouth.

"Cover her eyes," Sudan said, holding the flame protectively as she tried to roll from beneath his weight.

He touched the flame to the powder and a flash resulted. Despite both men's efforts, the girl's body arched up in pain. A muffled scream escaped from her bridled mouth. Sudan bit his own lip in sympathy.

Smoke and the stench of burning human flesh singed his nose. Both men coughed as they released her.

"Bad medicine," Rivers pronounced as he hurried outside.

Gently Sudan removed the leather from her slack mouth. Bending low, he listened to her breathing. The blackened wound no longer bled. Quickly he bandaged her shoulder. When he finished, he mopped her perspiring brow. Despite the cold, he was hot and sweaty. She seemed to be asleep or perhaps unconscious when he covered her with his blankets.

He rose and began changing his still wet clothes. He looked down at her over his shoulder and spoke softly to the semi-conscious girl.

"Comanche girl, I sure hope I don't live to regret shooting those bucks out there for you. But you are as pretty as any woman I ever saw."

Chapter Ten

The loggers were returning. Noble was pleased; he had missed the black man. Sudan seemed to be a closer link to the outside world than the Osage.

"He really can't come too quickly for me," Fleta said with shake of her head. "There isn't room in here to turn around." She stared at the stacks of store goods crowding the room. "I'll be glad to have the new additions completed."

"We'll get you more room. Maybe some more shelves, too," Noble promised, ignoring her irritability. He grimaced as he looked around. Fleta had a right to complain. As a living and working structure, the log cabin seemed to grow smaller each day.

He put on his hat. "I'll ride out and keep Sudan company."

"Do that, Noble," Fleta said with a stiff, but the twinkle in her eye belied her sour tone.

Noble admired her willowy form. He exchanged an intimate glance with her. At times, he couldn't believe that she belonged to him.

A little later, Noble reined up short of Sudan's procession. Rivers led a travois burdened horse. Noble studied it curiously. From his position, he could make out a human form in the sling, but since neither Rivers or Sudan was hurt—who was the injured person?

He rode close to Rivers. "Who's hurt?"

"A Comanche woman. Belongs to him," the Osage jerked a thumb in Sudan's direction.

"How's that?"

"Big battle. We win. New gun works good." Rivers held up the Winchester and grinned broadly.

Noble looked at the Osage and suppressed a shudder when he noticed the drying scalps dangling from Rivers' belt. He averted his eyes, wondering what the men were involved in. Well, at least they were back safely. He smiled.

The Osage nodded, clearly satisfied they had won over whatever enemy they had fought.

Noble reined the gray around so he could see who was in the travois. Their patient was awake, but did not acknowledge his presence. Her beauty startled Noble. Sudan had certainly found a rare flower. Apparently the woman was sick; her shoulder was bandaged but there was a small flicker of life in her that struck like flint.

Noble rode to the rear, mentally making an inventory of the logs, an impressive number. The oxen teams seemed trail-broken and were sledding along practically unguided.

"You've sure done great," Noble told Sudan with approval.

"I hope so." Sudan flashed his large white teeth in a grin. "You seen the woman?"

"Yes."

"Well, those new rifles sure spit out the bullets. I just hope we don't have any trouble at the fort over our battle. A band of Wichitas were after her. They'd wounded her."

Noble nodded absently, not quite clear about Sudan's story. "I'm glad the new rifles worked so well."

"Yep, they poured out them .44 slugs."

"And the woman. What's her name?" Noble asked quietly.

"I guess it's Gunsmoke for now," Sudan said with a heavy frown.

"Oh?" Noble wondered more about the incident. "What else?"

Sudan shrugged his massive shoulders. "Can't say. She ain't entirely a grateful person. Way I see it, them bucks aimed to kill her. She just don't care. She's all locked up inside or something."

"Maybe she'll come around," Noble said, trying to reassure his friend.

"I hope so. Rivers gave her the name Gunsmoke. We had to stop her from bleeding to death so I burned some gunpowder in the wound."

Noble's brows raised. "That worked?"

"Whew, yes. I sure hope she gets better, cause she is one pretty woman."

Both men laughed as they moved toward the fort. It was good to hear the blacksmith's loud booming voice again. The logs he brought would be a big start for Fleta's addition. In time, the problem of the Comanche woman's apathy would be resolved. Still, Noble had an inkling there could be trouble because of her.

At the fort, Mannah took charge of Gunsmoke. Rivers and the Osage men held a talk about the scalps. Sudan broke it up to get them to help unharness and unyoke the teams.

Fleta joined Noble on the porch. "What's wrong with the woman they brought in?"

"Wounded."

She tapped her foot impatiently. "I can see that."

"She seems to be very unhappy. I guess she misses her people," Noble said with a shrug.

Fleta watched the Indians working around the oxen. A shudder passed through her. "Those scalps that Rivers has. They make me—"

"Never mind," Noble interrupted her. "Come on inside." Noble shook his head behind her back. "That's just his way of bragging."

"Well, I don't like it, do you?" She paused to study Noble, who was frowning at something happening outside. "What is it?"

"Just checking." Noble noticed that a Wichitas had joined the men. How would they take his men's actions? Apparently, Rivers and Sudan had tangled with some of the Wichita's tribesmen. He sighed silently. There was no need to upset Fleta by telling her about it. He would just have to keep an eye out and stay close to the fort until he saw which way the wind would blow.

Noble felt certain that the Wichitas were planning something. Twice he drew Spotted Horse aside, but the Osage could not or would not say what the camp outside was thinking. On the second day after Sudan's return, Noble stopped Luke as he started to ride out the gate. "Luke, I want you to ride in the fort today."

"Why?" The boy looked at him with a frown.

"You just help Sudan today," he said curtly. His words and grim expression were enough to impress the importance of his instructions to Luke. Crestfallen, the boy turned his pony around and rode back to the stables. Noble realized how the boy felt, but the pending breech in the peace between the Osage and the Wichitas took precedence.

"Noble, is something wrong? Is there some kinda trouble?" Fleta asked from behind him.

He turned slowly, measuring his words before he spoke. "I'm not sure. I'm just being cautious."

She twisted her hands together. Why had he ordered Luke inside if nothing were wrong? "All right, Noble." It was an effort not to ask her husband more than that, but she forced back the words. Instead she turned and went back inside the store.

Later that afternoon, Chief Tall Timber, followed by several other Indians came through the gate in a procession. Noble watched them warily as he stood on the porch. When they halted a few yards short of him, he nodded a greeting, his muscles tense, a headache beginning at his temples.

"We have come to talk," the chief said slowly.

Noble agreed and they all started toward the open space near the wall. His footsteps felt leaden as he wondered what they wanted. Did they expect him to make some kind of decision or judgement? Hell, he didn't know a damn thing about Indian law.

They sat down on the ground in a council circle. Once seated, they looked at him expectantly.

From inside the store, Fleta watched the proceedings. Her nerves became taut with expectation. However the Wichitas did not look aggressive. Still...Noble was greatly outnumbered.

"Misses?"

She whirled, startled by Sudan who came in by the back door.

He was dressed in his buffalo coat and carried a rifle.

"What are they doing out there?" he asked, peering over her shoulder to look out the window.

"I-I'm not sure, Sudan."

"Humph! Maybe I better go out there." He started for the door, a repeater in his hand.

"Sudan, wait!" Fleta stopped him. "If Noble has trouble, we could help him more from in here."

Sudan scowled and stood silent for a moment. "Yes, ma'am. You could be right." He moved back to view the council from the window.

"Where's Luke?" Fleta asked abruptly, realizing that if her son was not with Sudan, he could be anywhere.

"Don't worry none, Misses. I left him busy doing a chore out back."

Fleta closed her eyes in silent prayer. Lord, please don't let anything happen.

The day was warmed by the sun. Noble sat cross legged, understanding only part of the oration and longing for a translator. The Wichita seated on either side of him grunted an occasional response to the chief's monologue.

As time crawled by on tense feet, Noble's irritation grew. Just what in the hell was going on. Were they plotting war or what? When his exasperation reached the stage of simmering anger, Noble shifted his position and prepared to do something—anything—to find out what the damned muttering was all about.

No-Eyes slipped up in front of him and squatted on his haunches. He peered at Noble with a deep frown. Noble grew rigid, knowing this was the moment he would find out what was going on with the enigmatic Indians.

"Noble," No-Eyes said softly, "What the Wichitas have said is that someone must take this chief's wives. Now that he has gone to his ancestors place, the Osage must take his women."

Noble looked at him blankly, wondering what the hell he was talking about. Then slowly, it began to dawn on him—this chief that Rivers and Sudan had killed in battle had *wives*. Noble had a hard time keeping a sober face looking at No-Eyes. The fact they expected someone to assume responsibility for the dead man's harem was a long ways from the threat Noble expected.

With great effort to keep a straight face, he asked. "Does Rivers accept them?"

No-Eyes shook his head. "They should belong to a chief."

Noble glanced around. All the Wichitas looked at him expectantly, waiting for him to make a decision for them. Apparently, they wanted him to act as their judge. He frowned thoughtfully.

"You mean, that Spotted Horse should take them?"

No-Eyes nodded.

"But Rivers has no wife," Noble said patiently. Hell, he didn't think Spotted Horse would thank him for adding to his household. He waited while No-Eyes interpreted his offer.

The Indians began another slow exchange. Noble scratched his neck idly. How much longer was this going to last? The sun was almost behind the west wall, which meant the air would be rapidly cooling. Anyway his legs were becoming stiff from sitting cross legged.

All at once he noticed all the affirmative head nods. Noble smothered a sigh of relief. He didn't need the Wichita to know they were accepting his idea.

Across the circle one of the men was preparing the pipe. A brave, wearing buffalo horns, rose and began to prance around the inside circle. Noble was sure the brave was not fully a man for his steps and motions were those of a woman. The buffalo horned dancer disgusted him, but his role was obviously an important part of the ceremony. The Wichitas on both sides of him leaned forward to listen intently to the prancing brave's chant.

After the smelly pipe was passed three times, the Wichitas began to disperse.

Spotted Horse came over to where Noble was trying to limber up his legs. Sudan joined them a moment later.

"Well, what's going on?" the black man asked, his eyes watching the departing Indians.

"They had to decide who got the dead chief's wives," Noble grumbled.

"They didn't mean Gunsmoke?" Sudan looked fiercely at them.

Spotted Horse shook his head. "Not your women. Rivers now gets two wives."

"Is that what this whole ruckus has been about?" Sudan asked.

Noble started to laugh. "How's old Rivers going to take all this?"

Spotted Horse shrugged. "Too many Wichitas to kill all of them. So he takes two wives." The Osage laughed; Noble and Sudan joined him.

Noble shook his head in bewilderment. He'd never understand the Indian's ways. The serious counciling was their court of law. Poor Rivers now acquired the dead man's obligation. Noble walked stiffly to the store, he had lots to tell Fleta.

River's brides arrived on a snowy day in December. Chief Beaver Tail's estate included twenty horses, five dogs and four children. Low Cow was a squat fat woman with diamond eyes. She wore beads and silver conchos. The second wife was Tall Cow—over six foot in height, she was thin with a very long neck. She nursed a young baby.

The names suited them. Noble hid a smile as Low Cow's sharp tongue berated Rivers for some misdemeanor. Poor River's bachelor days were over with a vengeance. Two more tepees were raised in the compound.

Winter promised to be a slow season. The first snow melted and left a thick quagmire of mud.

Noble was busy saddling his horse to ride out and check on the livestock when he heard a sharp wail and turned to see Low Cow emerge naked from her tepee. Her ponderous brown breasts bounced off her egg shaped belly as she ran. Behind her, Rivers came with a quirt, lightly flicking it at her brown buttock every few steps. The woman yelped as if she was mortally wounded. Noble watched the spectacle with an amused grin. Grunting as he ran, Rivers reached out to strike her. She placed her hands behind her for protection, her stubby legs threatening to buckle beneath her.

"Noble, stop them!" Fleta shouted, her expression outraged as she ran to him.

Noble caught her. "This is a private matter between Rivers and his wife." He bent and whispered in Fleta's ear, "Besides he's not hurting her."

Fleta was not to be mollified. She squirmed out of his arms, her eyes blazing as she glared at him. "Make him quit!"

"No." Noble looked down at her, admiring her flushed cheeks and sparkling eyes. "They have to resolve it themselves." He pulled her resisting body into his arms, knowing that when she was so fired up she might run in and interfere.

The other Osages were outside now, laughing as Low Cow sat in the mud, cowering from her husband. Rivers spoke loudly, the quirt held menacingly over her head. After a few more minutes of angry verbal abuse, Rivers turned and stalked back to his tepee. His wife pushed up and without a sideways glance, hurried after him. A moment later, she reappeared wrapped in a blanket, carrying Rivers' trophy staff. With a distasteful look at the staff, which was decorated with scalps—including her own husband's—she stuck it in the ground outside the tepee's opening.

Noble realized he still had his own wife in his arms. "I think it's settled now."

Fleta backed out of his arms, her face full of disapproval. "Well, I certainly hope so."

Noble smiled at her tight-lipped expression. "Fleta, I would never do that to you," he said with a smothered laugh.

Fleta's face flushed with anger. "And I would never let you!" She turned and flounced back toward the store.

Sudan sauntered over to Noble and grinned at him. "Whew! I thought you'd get whipped."

Noble glanced at his wife's retreating shape. He shook his head. "Not this time."

Sudan chuckled, then became serious. "Noble, I have the wagon ready to go to Independence whenever you're ready."

"Fine." Noble wasn't eager to leave. Word was out that the Cheyenne and Sioux were becoming belligerent and aggressive, west of the fort.

His role as head of the fort was a complicated one. He was expected to make decisions for the Indians, keep the store supplied with goods, watch that wolves didn't cut down his growing herd of cattle, keep the Wichitas happy, and cope with whatever other problems cropped up. Plus, Captain Rourke obviously expected him to keep an eye out for trouble from other Indian tribes. Well, at least he owned the land now. That was one problem resolved. Perhaps someday he would get the area surveyed and permanently marked.

"Something wrong, Noble?" Sudan asked.

"No, nothing I can't handle," he said wryly. "How's Gunsmoke?"

Sudan shook his head sadly. "She's healing, but not in the mind."

Maybe the Comanche woman would recover, Noble mused. Who wouldn't, with the company of a man like Sudan. Noble hoped the woman would start to act more lifelike, for Sudan's sake, but it seemed that was not to be.

"I need to take her back home," Sudan said regretfully.

Noble looked at the man sharply, not wanting his friend to leave again. "Where's her home?"

"West Texas, I think. I ain't having no one feeling like they're my slave."

"Yes, you're probably right, Sudan. I'm sorry. It could be a long, tough journey. The country's full of war-like tribes."

"Yes, sir. But if I don't take her back, she'll die before spring. She ain't a woman while she's staying here; she ain't nothing."

Noble nodded his understanding. "Whenever you get ready to go, take the supplies and whatever you need. We'll miss you, Sudan, but I think I understand."

Sudan looked at Noble with a smile of relief. He stuck out his big, calloused hand. "Thank you, Noble McCurtain. You're a fine man." They shook hands gravely. "Guess I'll go on and get ready to leave now. Won't gain nothing by putting it off."

"Yes." Noble turned and walked toward the store. Would the black man survive a trip so far away, one filled with potential danger?

That night as they lay in bed, Noble told Fleta of Sudan's problems and his plans to take the woman home.

"I'll get more boards in Independence to finish the addition to the house," he said, abruptly changing the subject.

She pressed her body against his. "That'll be good. I'll miss Sudan. He's a comforting person to have around. It's a shame that Gunsmoke can't see what a good and gentle man he is."

"Yeah, a damned shame," Noble said with feeling.

They lay in silence for a while. Fleta ran the tip of her tongue over her lips, wanting to ask Noble something, yet afraid of what he might say. Her hand went to her flat stomach, and bitterness tears welled in her eyes. It was so unfair.

"Noble," she whispered hesitantly, "Noble, why can't I get pregnant? Has God cursed me for leaving Wilbourne? Is this some kind of punishment?" Tears squeezed beneath her lashes as she felt him stiffen beside her. Oh, why had she said anything?

"Fleta," he said on a deeply expelled breath. "God has not cursed you."

"He must have."

Noble's lips tightened when he realized he must tell her the truth. Groaning, he put his arm around her and pulled her closer so he could look into her eyes. Then he pressed his forehead to her cheek.

"I'm sorry, Fleta. It's my fault, I should have told you sooner..." He paused, uncertain of the right words.

Fleta blinked in the dim light from the fireplace. What was he talking about? "Noble, I don't—"

"Shh. Let me explain. I couldn't tell you before, I didn't want to risk losing you. Fleta, I had a bad case of mumps years ago. The doctor told me...I'm the one who can't produce children, sweetheart. Not you."

Fleta was silent with shock. She would never know the joy of having Noble's seed growing inside her. Oh, it was so unfair.

She spoke her thoughts aloud, "Oh, Noble, you need a son."

"I have Luke," he said with a smile. "He's a good boy, Fleta. I couldn't ask for a finer son. But what about you? Do you want to leave me—a man who can't even give you children?" he asked in a hoarse whisper.

Yes, he did have Luke, she assured herself. As for her leaving him...She placed her hand alongside his jaw and smiled tenderly. "Oh, Noble, I would never leave you. Why didn't you tell me sooner? I've worried myself sick, thinking I was unable to give you a child."

"Well, I guess you never asked," he said with a smile.

She raised up on her elbow and looked down into his face.

Tenderly she placed a kiss against his mouth.

With trembling fingers, Noble gathered the hem of her nightgown and pulled it upward. "As long as I have you, I don't care about anything else, Fleta."

Chapter Eleven

Sudan rode out the front gate, the winter sun on his wooly black head, two pack horses in tow behind him. His woman, Gunsmoke, seemed oblivious to the well wishers as she followed on her horse.

In his buffalo coat, the black man looked strong, capable of taking care of himself. Noble watched him leave with a slight frown. He didn't even hear Fleta, so engrossed was he in the black man's departure.

"Sudan will be all right," she assured him, taking a hold of his arm to gain his attention. Noble smiled down on her. In the past she had pulled him out of a lot of moods by attaching herself to him as she was doing now.

"I agree," he said, "but he's going into a mighty inhospitable world."

"He wants Gunsmoke happy."

Noble rubbed a hand through his hair. "I know, Fleta. I just hate to lose him. Not only is he a good worker, but he's become a close friend."

"I know, Noble. Come back inside, I'll brew some fresh tea."

"Nothing I can do now." He circled her shoulder and they went back inside the store.

Sudan was uncertain of the future as he headed out on his journey. He had the new repeater, a cap and ball Colt Noble gave him, and enough ammunition to last a while. But his new woman worried him more than any unknown trouble ahead. The beautiful Comanche woman, so supple and lovely, seemed to him like she was dead inside. Nothing he did for her or to her raised even a spark of life. She just accepted his advances. Finally in disgust, he began to sleep alone. He was angry because he couldn't awaken her womanhood, yet he was not so desperate as to take an unwilling woman.

The days grew warmer as they crossed the short grass land, bisected with fewer streams. He avoided Indian camps and the larger buffalo herds.

Sudan shot a small deer for their meat. He noticed the woman working the hide as they rode. He shifted his eyes to the brown sea of short grass, for he knew if he looked at her, he would be tempted by her physical beauty.

He had no idea how much further he must travel. There was nothing—no trees, no hills, just open grass prairie. Gunsmoke rode beside him and handed him a buckskin fringed scabbard for his rifle. He frowned suspiciously at her gift.

"Now that sure is pretty," he said aloud, admiring the fringed cover.

She rose in the stirrups and pointed southwest. Sudan blinked at her. A smile was flickering at the corner of her mouth and a light sparkled in her brown pupils.

They were five days out of Noble's Fort. Sudan sighed wryly at the abrupt change in the woman. Either the bad water they'd been drinking hit her or the good Lord had silently struck her. His spirits rose as he pushed the oily barrel into the deerhide sheath. Certainly he was not going to worry about what caused the damage. He was too elated.

Sudan caught sight of something that caused some of his euphoria to fade. Specks appeared in the distance. He was certain they weren't buffaloes. White, red, and brown animals meant Indian ponies. Far on the western horizon, the ponies rode on a parallel course with his. How long had they been out there?

"Are they Comanches?" he asked, knowing she had spotted the riders, too.

"No."

How in the hell could she tell at that distance? he wondered. She was Indian enough to know, he supposed. They were moving fast, which meant there were no women and travois with them. They, no doubt, had already spotted him and his pack train.

What he needed was a place to hole up. Out here that might not be easy to do. He had turned to look at the east when Gunsmoke let out a yip and rode off toward the west.

Girl, Sudan said silently, if you aim to leave me for them . . . She reined up and signaled for him to join her. He kicked his horse in the ribs and jerked the pack horse lead line.

She'd found a buffalo wallow. Sudan judged it to be thirty feet across and six feet deep in the center. Gunsmoke charged her horse down the steep bank. Reining in sharply, she dismounted and grinned up at him.

"Yes, ma'am. You have parted the Red Sea, girl. Just like Moses did." Sudan gave a last look to the west as he went over the steep bank. He could not see the enemy.

Gunsmoke hobbled their horse while he climbed up the side with his rifle. The sun's sinking rays fired the prairie with golden red glares that obscured his enemy.

She joined him, scrambled up on top, then lay her ear to the ground.

"No come," she said and twisted to dangle her brown legs over the edge. The smile of satisfaction on her face stirred him. "Good place. They come at dawn."

"Guess we'll have to give them a real welcome," Sudan said, setting his full lips together firmly. He stared in amazement at the change in his woman. She was sparkling with life. He frowned fiercely. "Come on," he said, afraid of his growing desire for her. He started back to the horses where she joined him. They shared water from one of the water bags. The horses had muddied the stale water in the pit. At least he noted they had a drink. He rationed out a handful of cornmeal in their nose bags, wanting the horses to be rested and fed since he and Gunsmoke might need them to flee this place.

As he filled each bag, she put them on the horses. Their chomping was loud in the still twilight. Sudan kept listening, but he couldn't detect any other sounds.

After completing the chores for the horses, he left them saddled, then he and Gunsmoke climbed up on the rim, taking some dried jerky and blankets with them. Seated on the grass in the fast cooling last glow of day, they chewed on the hard meat.

When Gunsmoke finished eating, she moved in front of him and rubbed a grease slicked finger on his mouth. He licked the smokey salt flavor and watched as she calmly sat back down. He could fathom no reason for her action unless she was feeling affectionate.

Then Gunsmoke placed a blanket over his shoulders and moved close by his side. Sudan realized for the first time that she belonged to him. But the stirring in his flanks melted at the sounds of distant war drums.

The Indians were working up their nerve, clearing things with their gods. Wails and sharp cries carried across the prairie.

"Kiowas," she said, snuggling close to him.

"Kiowas," he repeated. "Are they bad?"

He saw her head bob. If she figured they were, he expected the worst. Indians usually underestimated their enemies. Well, they were up against a determined man.

Sudan dozed a few minutes before he jerked awake. It was quiet. The Indians had either exhausted themselves or were sneaking up on them. When he shifted to look across the starlit plains, Gunsmoke awoke.

Reassuringly, she patted his leg. "We shoot plenty Kiowas."'

"Can you shoot a pistol?" he asked, not convinced the Kiowas weren't already sneaking up on their bellies nearby.

She pulled the Colt out of his waistband and held it steady. "Bang."

"I don't have much time for a lesson," Sudan said dryly.

She aimed the pistol out in the night, clicked the hammer back, and the pistol roared. The fiery orange flames flashed out the barrel. Sudan nodded.

"Girl, you are a wonder." He hugged her warmly. "Now let me reload that chamber." Sudan took the pistol and held it up to reload the powder and ball, replacing the cap on the nipple. He gave the pistol back.

"Kiowas, you ain't never run up against a tougher pair," he said smugly.

He awoke the second time when she tugged on his arm. Sudan drew a deep breath. How long had he slept? he wondered. It must be close to dawn. There was a little gray seam on the horizon.

They slipped into the wallow. His pockets weighted with the brass cartridges, he pulled off the carbine's fringed holster. A south wind swept his face as he dug out shells and placed them on the top of the bank. He was grateful the breeze would carry off the powder smoke so he could see them. Sudan laid the rifle on the bank. Come on, you howling devils, I'm ready.

Dawn cracked on the horizon and he saw the distant outline of riders. He checked on Gunsmoke; she was resting her elbows on the bank, the Colt in both hands. He wanted to warn her not to waste ammunition, but was afraid if he spoke he would break her concentration.

Then he felt the vibration of running horses beneath his elbows. The earth shook, warscreams slit the air as the Kiowas came. He sighted into the glaring sun at their outlines, squinting his eyes down the bead.

The air filled with the 'yi-yi' war cries now. Sudan judged the range; his rifle cracked and a Kiowa tumbled off his pony. A second round had another one down. The third took a pony. Four rounds and they swerved to the north. Sudan rose and dropped a red and white pony; the rider jumped up, but Gunsmoke's pistol blasted him. Hit squarely by the ball, the buck arched his back. He staggered until he pitched face down.

The party was well out of the rifle's range when they pulled up. Sudan quickly reloaded, his breath coming in gulps. From the corner of his eye, he saw something that made him stop his rapid actions.

"Get back here!" he shouted. Busy and bent low Gunsmoke was gathering bows, arrows, and lances. What the hell did she think she was doing? He glanced to the enemy regrouping and yelling. A sigh of relief escaped him as she raced back, dumped the armload and jumped into the pit.

"What are we going to do with them?" he asked, looking from her to the weapons on the side of the slope.

She just smiled and nodded proudly. "More Kiowas."

"Yeah," he said wryly, turning back.

The Kiowas charged again. Screaming, they came in a long line of low riders, shooting muzzle loaders and arrows.

The Winchester spoke and a horse screamed, going end over end, smashing its rider.

Arrows swished, pinpricking the ground around them. One tucked at Sudan's sleeve. He was satisfied that it had only pierced his coat. He fired again and again, at times hitting a rider or a horse. With wonder, he noticed that Gunsmoke was shooting a bow and arrow.

She struck a Kiowa horse in the neck. His rider fled afoot unscathed, despite two .44/.40 rounds sent in his direction. The buck was rescued by another who swept in. Her final arrow sent a pinto—struck in the hind quarter—into a bucking fit.

The rifle barrel was hot, the heated oil smelled burnt. He reloaded as she quickly gathered more arrows.

"We're going to hold them," he said.

"Yes, we will," she said so perfectly and so confidently he had to smile.

Sweet Jesus, she could talk English if she wanted to. He wondered what else she would do to shock him? He admired her grit; she made a helluva ally.

The Kiowa were coming back, head on. Suicide! They began their charge. Spent powder burned his nose, his eyes smarted, tears streaked down his black face. His throat begged for a drink of anything wet.

Screaming like mad men, the Indians came at the wallow. Sudan fired, piling horses and Indians, still they continued to come. Gunsmoke's arrows took a toll, but three Kiowas were left when the Winchester fell on an empty chamber. He started to reload.

"Sudan!" she shouted, ready with a lance for him.

He dropped the rifle and caught the shaft. Driving it upward into the rider that leaped over him, he threw himself aside. Intended for him, a spear struck into the bank. He jerked it out of the ground and whirled.

A great scream escaped his mouth as he thrust the spear up with all his force into the belly of the horse above him. The rider fell into the pit and scrambled lithely to his feet in time for Sudan to implant the stone point of the spear into his breast work of quills.

A pistol shot caused him to whirl around as the last fighter fell beside him. The dead Indian's knife arm was outstretched ready to pounce on Sudan.

Gunsmoke gave him a quick glance then scrambled up the bank.

He grabbed the Winchester and jammed shells into the receiver. Were there any Kiowas left?

Her pistol roared and another Kiowa was down. Out of breath, Sudan searched the field of dead men and horses. He frowned at Gunsmoke gathering up the remaining live horses. Proudly she delivered them to him.

"Well, gal, at least we ain't horse poor," he said, taking the reins. She was gone again, her brown legs flashing below her calf length buckskin skirt.

He sat down and scratched the side of his curly head. Mr. Lincoln set me free, he mused. Maybe the Kiowas had done that for Gunsmoke. He wasn't certain about much, except that the battle was over and they'd won.

He had no desire to sit amongst a bunch of dead Indians. Sudan rose to his feet and led his string of war horses—which she had collected—south of the wallow. After he had picketed them, he took Gunsmoke's and his own horses to put with the others.

His thirst quenched with water from the canvas bag, Sudan gnawed on a piece of jerky and watched the woman. He blinked as he realized she was skinning one of the dead horses. He supposed she had a purpose behind her actions.

"Gunsmoke, ain't you in a hurry to get home?" He joined her and drew out his big knife to help.

She paused and shook her head. "My name is Yellow Deer. We go back to your smelly tepee. Yellow Deer will make a new tepee with these hides. When it smells bad, we move."

"Gawdamighty! We could have done that before," he said slicing the hide from the carcass. "Yellow Deer, huh?"

"Yellow Deer."

"Well hell. Here I've killed fourteen Kiowas, four Wichitas and Lord knows how many ponies to find out that your name is Yellow Deer. How many hides do we need?" When she didn't answer, he put a hand on her arm to get her attention. "How many?"

She smiled slyly. "All of the dead ones."

He shook his head and bent back to his chore. Her hand stopped him and he looked at her questioning.

"Yellow Deer will do this, Sudan."

"No. We both will."

"Good." She smiled at him in approval.

Sudan shed his coat. The rising sun was growing hot. He sighed with resignation. Heaven only knew what else she would want to collect before they left. Sudan felt proud, working shoulder to shoulder with her as they finished skinning the first horse.

"You are a plenty good man." She gave him a bump with her hip and rose up to stretch her back.

With a great effort, Sudan rolled the half-peeled horse over. "There must be five more horses. Are you sure we need all of them?"

She nodded and resumed her skinning. When Sudan glanced up at her, they exchanged a silent look of challenge. Wordlessly they raced to finish the skinning.

He intended to be miles away from this place by nightfall. Ghosts or no ghosts, he wanted no part of the Kiowa spirits.

"Five more?" he repeated, but she didn't answer.

By sundown, they were loaded with beadwork, Kiowa head-dresses, silver conchoes, and copper jewelry. A bundle of lances, bows and arrows, even buffalo-hide shields and a half dozen muzzle loaders were added to their bounty. Sudan was relieved she hadn't scalped or mutilated any of the corpses.

His arms aching, Sudan was glad to ride away from the fly-infested death scene at last. The smell of butchered horses was heavy in his nose as he turned his horse toward home. Yellow Deer whipped the laggards with a Kiowa quirt while he led them.

When daylight began to fade and the warmth of the sun followed Sudan and the woman stopped to camp at a small stream. After unpacking all their new wealth and hobbling the horses, they walked down to the stream.

He washed his hands and beard-stubbled face. Free of the remaining stiff blood, he dried his hands on a kerchief. Wearily, he raised up, still amazed that he and his woman had survived a battle with the suicidal Kiowas.

"Sudan!" she called, unfurling the bedroll.

He frowned, wondering what she was up to. Then a slow smile spread over his mouth. She wiggled out of her deerskin dress for him. He felt revitalized as he walked toward her. His eyes locked on her bronze body, bathed in the red sunset's last spears.

Sudan started to undress, his eyes never leaving hers.

Out checking on his livestock, Noble had been studying the dust of a herd of horses on the move for over an hour. It might be Sudan returning. The direction was right, but why would the black man have so many horses? He waited patiently, his mind roaming at will. How long had the black man been gone? Two weeks.

Noble stood in the stirrups and squinted. The unmistakable rider in the lead was the giant black man. Who did he have with him? And where in hell did he get all those horses? When he dropped back in the saddle, Noble shook his head in wonder. It didn't matter; it was enough to know Sudan was returning unharmed.

Noble raced the stallion to meet him. A good feeling spread through Noble as he rode. Sudan was back. They greeted each other with wide smiles and handshakes.

Noble looked over the pack string behind Sudan. "You sure brought a lot of stuff. The Comanches give you all this?"

"Kiowas," Sudan waved to the rider in the back of the pack. "Remember Gunsmoke?" he asked Noble. "Her real name is Yellow Deer."

"Hello, Mr. Noble," she said shyly, keeping her eyes averted from Noble's.

"Yes, hello," Noble said in surprise. It was the same woman, all right, but the woman he knew as Gunsmoke would never have spoken to him. Why, she'd hardly even said a word to Fleta.

"She has enough horse hides to make a new tepee for us. We even cut poles along the way to use for our new home," Sudan said with a proud smile at Yellow Deer.

Noble looked from the woman to the black man. "I wish you both much happiness."

"Thank you, Mr. Noble." Sudan winked. "Let's go, Yellow Deer. We need to get home."

"Home," she repeated and actually smiled at Noble.

He sat for a moment in bewilderment, then fell in beside Sudan. There were things in life a man wasn't supposed to know. The change in a woman was one of them. He had to remember her real name, Noble reminded himself. He silently repeated "Yellow Deer."

Chapter Twelve

In the spring of 1867, Fleta waited for the first wagon train customers to push west. The Wichitas had already moved south to intercept their brother, the buffalo. She reflected a moment. At eleven years, Luke seemed far too old for his age. Noble was no help to her either, encouraging her son to try grown up things.

Sudan had long since finished the house additions, twice put aside for warehouse room constructions. At least their bed no longer fell under every customer's scrutiny. Now their talks and love making were accomplished discreetly behind a closed door. It was a comforting fact that freed her from any fear that some Indian might barge in at the very peak of their passion.

All the Indian women were pregnant, except Yellow Deer and Mannah.

"Will we catch the Santa Fe trail on west?" a big man in patched suit asked her one day in the store.

"You'd best ask my husband," she said as she added up his order.

"Yes ma'am. Say didn't that Injun woman call you Fleta?"

"Yes." She looked up at the man, wondering why he was so curious about her name.

The man scratched his sideburns and looked undecided. "Well, I was in the war in '64 with a man by the name of Wilbourne Corey. He had a wife by that name. Never heard it before. Coincidence, ain't it?"

She hoped her face had not paled. Her lips pursed together, she shook her head and mumbled, "McCurtain is my last name."

"Didn't that Corey man live in Arkansas?" the man's wife asked.

"Yes, but this lady doesn't have time to listen to your patter. Pay her for the geehaws."

Fleta wanted to run and hide. She had not even thought about Wilbourne Corey in a long, long time. Now it bothered her to think about his lonely return to the empty cabin. She also knew if Noble hadn't joined them, she and Luke would never have survived.

It was an effort to stay in the store, waiting on customers the rest of the day. She was tempted to leave the store in Mannah's hands and rush out to the bedroom to hide. But that would be cowardly and she would not be guilty of such action. She loved Noble and it was her place to clerk the store. Fortunately, she was able to work up a small amount of confidence. Yet, the day passed slowly. She had to recheck her additions on bills of goods, apologizing to a nameless face when she discovered her mistake.

That evening she still left anxious. As she washed dishes, her mind wandered. A fork fell from her fingers on the floor.

"Damnit!" she swore softly.

Noble looked up from his tea. "What's wrong?"

"Nothing."

"If it's nothing, then why are you irritated?"

"It has been a tiring day."

"I'll hire you a clerk."

"I don't need any more help. Mannah and I nearly fall over each other."

"I'll make the store bigger."

She looked at the ceiling for strength. "Noble McCurtain, can't I have one bad day?"

"Yes." He looked at her worriedly. "People are sure early this year. The grass isn't even green and they're pushing west with eagerness written on their faces."

"Hmm," Fleta mumbled as she bent to check on her biscuits.

"The further west they go, the less enthusiasm they'll have, for they won't have forage for their livestock."

She slammed the pan of biscuits on the rangetop. "Oh, damn!"

"What's damned now? Did you burn yourself?"

Hands on her hips, she glared at him. "No, the biscuits. I'm just tired. Oh!'' She tore off her apron and stalked out through the store. After wrestling with the stubborn latch, she went on the porch and out in the yard to vent her anger.

The Osage men frowned at her from their positions in front of the tepees. They sat in their store bought clothes, rifles across their laps. Nothing escaped their eyes, especially hard case customers who drifted in from time to time. Their armed and alert presence was enough to make any would-be troublemaker pay and leave peacefully.

Spotted Horse rose and walked over to her. ''Misses, when the buffalo come, we will feast on tongue and hump.''

''Yes,'' she said, her mood melting away in the cool evening air.

''They will come soon and chase away the worry of winter.''

''I think it would help. We're ready for spring.''

He nodded and exchanged a warm smile with her before he returned to the others.

''Mama?'' Luke called. ''Noble has the food ready. Are you coming to eat now?''

''Yes, Luke. I'm coming.'' Maybe fresh buffalo meat would help her. She glanced at the Indians as she went toward the house. They were such simple yet complicated people. Spotted Horse had known when she was upset. But he had not asked why. That was an Indian's way though. Their philosophy was to take their minds off their current problems. What problems? She sighed and went to rejoin her family.

A slow uneventful week passed. Three riders came in for tobacco and candy. They were polite young men, almost awkward in her presence.

''We're going to Color-ado,'' one said, almost as if he expected praise.

''That's nice,'' Fleta said with a smile.

''Ma'am?''

''Yes?''

''Guess it wouldn't insult you if I took the liberty to say . . . well, you sure are purty.''

''Thank you,'' Fleta said demurely, feeling the color flood her cheeks.

The young man sauntered off, a little hesitantly to the door.

"I mean it," he said, snatching off his floppy hat.

"Yes. Thank you."

She almost laughed aloud after he left. Alone at last, she decided to work on the books. Mannah was straightening shelves.

"Where's Luke?" Fleta asked.

"With Sudan."

"Learning how to kill Kiowas, I suppose," she said pensively.

"No. Sudan does not boast. They are probably working on iron things."

Fleta nodded. Purty, he had said. The poor boy must have vision problems. She set the pen down. Noble would be back soon from checking his stock. Maybe she should brush her hair and tie it back with a ribbon. The books could wait.

She stopped at a pecking sound on the roof. "Is it raining?"

"Yes," Mannah said.

The rain increased. Fleta began brushing her hair, worrying about her man. Perhaps she should call Luke in. And where was Noble? A grumble of thunder caused her to frown. She certainly hoped it wasn't going to storm.

Luke burst in the back door. "It's raining, mama."

"I know. Don't track up my clean floors," she warned, proud of the smooth wood.

"Is Noble back?" Luke asked, looking around.

"No."

"Funny, he usually comes in before the rain."

"I know." She winced as she dragged the brush through her tangled hair. "He'll be along."

Fleta sent Mannah home and she looked out in the gray wet world of splattered puddles. Where was he?

Reluctantly, she went back to feed Luke. Noble's dinner would stay warm in the oven.

Noble came in, dripping water all over the floor. "Sorry, I'm late."

"Get out of those wet clothes. You'll catch a death of cold. Why did you stay so long out in the rain?"

"Rustlers," he said grimly. "They've stolen several of our horses. I lost their tracks. Come sunup, I intend to be on their trail."

"It may still be raining," she said as she helped him undress.

"Then I'll wear an oilskin poncho. Doesn't matter, I'm going after them. I haven't worked to gather a band of horses only to have them stolen."

"Where did they take them?" she asked, hanging the sodden clothing on a line she used inside.

"Indian Territory."

"Indians?"

He shook his head and smiled at Luke who came in the store. "You all right, Luke?"

"Yes," he said. "Is my name McCurtain or Corey?"

Fleta looked at Noble, her eyes round with shock. Where on earth had Luke come up with that kind of question?

Noble gave Luke a direct look. "Your name is Luke McCurtain."

"Well, that's what I told the lady from the wagon train."

Fleta met Noble's questioning look and hastily explained. "A man who was in the war with Wilbourne heard Mannah mention my name. He recalled hearing it from Wilbourne. His wife must have asked Luke."

"Damned nosy people! Where are they camped? Is it that bunch west of the store?"

"Noble, please, there is no reason for you to be upset. They're just curious, I guess."

He shrugged and went to find some clean dry clothes. His jaw clenched, he raged against people who pried into other's business. Still upset, he sat on the bed and began pulling off his wet boots.

"Noble McCurtain," Fleta said from the doorway. "I am not going to ever leave you. Not ever."

Noble smiled and studied his toes. "Sorry, this horse thieving has me all wrought up."

"I know."

"I do all these things for you and Luke," he said uncertainly.

"And we appreciate you." Fleta walked into his arms and leaned her head against his chest.

Noble smoothed her hair. He was thinking about the rustlers, but was warmed by the bond between Fleta and himself. She was pleased to share a private moment after a hard day; still the fact that he was leaving again worried her.

Luke came bursting in to tell Noble about his welding two pieces of iron to repair a rim that Sudan had found on the prairie.

"Bound together like a wedding ring," Noble said softly.

Fleta was filled with love by Noble's quiet words. To hide the threat of emotional tears, she scowled at her son's grubby appearance. "You're late. Go wash your hands. Right now, young man!"

"But, Mama, I had to finish it. Didn't I Noble?"

He agreed with the boy and received a silent look of reproach from the Fleta. She left to check on her food in the oven. Someone had abandoned the stove at the side of the road and like so many other nice pieces of furniture, Noble packed it in. She drew the pans out of the oven, her face bathed in the heat from the fire. Why did everything have to be a reminder? She closed her eyes for a moment, hoping the feeling of depression would pass.

Later, in bed, Noble's gentle hands massaged her into a state of readiness. His hungry mouth on her neck, hair and face melted her depression. She responded to him with an abandon that secretly shocked her. He took her with a sweetness that wiped out all her regrets and guilt. She loved Noble more than anything else in the world.

Rain played on the roof when they awoke. Luke had built a fire in the range. He had awakened early with a small spark of hope that Noble would take him along when he rode out to chase down the horse thieves. He suspected the answer would be no, but he would be ready just in case. Prepared for the negative, Luke handed Noble the Winchester wrapped in canvas.

"Thanks, Luke," Noble said, a little confused as to why the boy was up and making a fire.

"I sort of thought that Shaw and I could ride along with you, Noble."

"Oh?" Noble considered the prospect. "I think you'd better stay here this time. I need someone here to help your mother and Sudan." He patted the boy's shoulder in sympathy.

"Sure, Noble," Luke said, his face crestfallen.

When Spotted Horse joined Noble at the gate, the Osage wore an oil slicker, using it as a poncho against the rain. Fleta watched the men mount up with a feeling of foreboding. Noble waved and whirled the gray stallion around. With splashes of hooves and distant thunder, they rode out of the fort, the Osage dogs yapping after them.

Close to the Indian Territory line, Noble ducked his head so his hat could protect his face from the driving rain. Spotted Horse seemed convinced the horses had been driven in this direction even though the tracks had dissolved. By the second day, they were in small hills dotted with rock outcroppings and post oaks.

Everything was wet and soggy. They had cold camped the previous night, sleeping huddled in their rain gear, expecting and receiving more downpours.

The Osage was squatted beside a small swollen creek on the third day. He rose and waved Noble over to point out the deep water filled hoof tracks in the muddy ground.

"They are nearby."

Noble nodded. "I hope so. We must nearly be in Texas."

Spotted Horse shook his head. "Still plenty way."

Noble didn't argue. Every muscle in his body ached, the cold rain was taking its toll on him. How Spotted Horse could stand the weather and long ride without wearing down, was beyond him. Perhaps he rested in the saddle.

By evening, signs of the herd were evident. Noble found enough resolve in the unraveling events to wash out some of his weariness. His senses sharpened as he stood in the saddle to stretch and view the gray sundown.

"Tonight, we will sneak up on their camp," Spotted Horse said as they trotted their horses to be closer by darkness.

"I hope so." Noble nodded as he rode stirrup to stirrup with the Osage. The thieves would pay dearly for stealing his stock.

Under cover of darkness, the pair slipped up on the rustler's campfire. No one built a fire like that, Noble realized, not if they were suspecting someone on their back trail. Chilled as he was, he shivered, envious of their bright fire.

Spotted Horse moved to his right. Noble waited until the Osage had time to be in place. He drew the Colt out slowly and stepped forward.

"Hands high!" Noble ordered.

The flash of a pistol shocked him. He ducked, firing two quick rounds in the direction of the gunfire. Had he hit the enemy? He couldn't be sure. Dammed rustlers were going to fight it out. He rolled on his belly, a sharp pain in his right leg. Damn, was he hit?

This was the third day. She cringed at every roll of thunder over head. Rain streamed down the front window. Fleta peered between blasts, knowing that the huddled rider was not her husband.

A rider came though the gate, too bent over to be Noble. She was dismayed. The man dismounted clumsily and came to the door. He pushed inside without stomping his boots first.

Water ran off the scruffy stranger's oil cloth and pooled around his muddy boots on her polished floor. "Is there a man here with a team who can help some folks who are mired down east of here? They can pay him. I tried but my old horse couldn't budge them?"

"Certainly," Fleta said. "Go around in back. The blacksmith will go help them."

"I got to ride on, but I'm sure he'll be able to find them."

"Yes, well you just go tell him where they are stuck."

"Yes ma'am. I'll go tell him."

"He'll handle it." She opened the door and after the man left, looked disgusted at the mess he left behind. Oh, well, she thought of the poor stranded people who were probably beside themselves with worry, and admitted hers was a small nuisance.

Sudan stuck his bushy head in the front door. "I'm going to take the mares and ride up to help them folks. That fellow thought it be somewhere near Elder Bush Creek." He shook his head. "He sure didn't know directions."

"How's that?" Fleta's eyes narrowed.

"He said he never been around here before. Didn't know the name of the place they broke down at. Thought it was four or five miles back."

"You wear your rain coat," Fleta warned. "And you be careful."

"I will. Funny, I think I seen the man come by here before. He sure was messed up. I can't remember if he said they had oxen or horses.''

"I'm not sure he told me. Why?"

"Never mind. I think he said both," Sudan shrugged. "I got my oil cloth. It won't take me no time with them mares to pull them out.''

Fleta watched him mount the big mare. He rode out the gate, leading the team mate. The man was happy about the change in his Comanche wife, Yellow Deer. Mannah said that the woman had come to her senses in time. She would have been rejected by her people anyway.

At sundown, Fleta prepared to close up. Mannah was spending time with Mary Joseph whose second child was due anytime. Business had been slow all day. Sudan had not returned. Fleta surmised that either the wagon was mired down or further away than the man thought.

A rig turned in the yard at breakneck speed, nearly spilling the driver. "Mrs. McCurtain!" the driver shouted. Fleta fumbled with the new latch on the door, looking out at the man with a puzzled frown.

"Mrs. McCurtain?" the youth asked. Still another stranger. "Grab a cover. Your husband's been hurt bad.''

"Noble?" Fleta felt a wave of fear spreading through her. She clutched at the door's edge, her legs trembling beneath her.

"Yes ma'am . Come on," the wild-eyed youth said impatiently.

"Is he far?" Fleta asked, her mind frantically sifting through the possible injuries Noble might have suffered.

"A ways," the driver said with a shrug.

"Luke! Luke!" Fleta shouted as she raced back inside the store. She took a canvas coat from the stock. When her son appeared in the door to their quarters, she spoke sharply. "Go get Mannah. Have her close up the store and stay here. Noble's been hurt. I'll be back soon as I can.''

Luke's eyes shadowed with fear. "Is Noble hurt bad?"

Fleta bit her lip. "I'm not sure, Luke. Now do as I say; put the slicker on and go get Mannah.''

Fleta rushed outside. The stranger pulled her up on the seat. "Hang on!" he shouted then yelled to the team.

Fleta gripped the seat, holding on tightly as the team sped away. The hell-bent driver slapped the rain-slick horses, directing them out the gate toward the south.

If they didn't break a leg in a prairie dog hole, he surely would get her to Noble in record time. Rain washed her eyes as she jostled on the spring seat. Beside her, the bent over youth continued to whip the poor horses.

When he started down the long grade to a stream, he sawed the horses to slow them down. In the twilight, Fleta saw two riders ahead by the dimly lit road. She hoped they would tell her how Noble was.

His feet braced and half-standing, the driver stopped.

"Here she is!" he shouted.

Abruptly rough hands reached out and jerked Fleta out of the seat and held her belly-down over a masculine lap.

"Get going and keep going!" A gravely voice shouted.

"Yeah," the driver replied over the rain.

"What are you doing?" Fleta demanded as she fought to free herself from the imprisoning thick arms that pinned her. She was on a horse, lying over a man's lap, her nose pressed against the side of her captor's pant leg. She tried to look up at the tall man whose voice had a vague ring of familiarity. Cautiously she peered upward, tilting her head to see him in the dim light. Oh God! Izer Goodman!

Fleta groaned at her stupidity. There was nothing wrong with Noble. It was a ploy to kidnap her and she fell for it. Another groan escaped her as she realized that even the scruffy looking man who had wanted Sudan to pull some people out of the mire was a part of the plan. Anger raging through her, she struggled furiously with her captor. He subdued her easily, laughing with mockery as her body drained of strength.

"I got you, girl, and I'm taking you where he'll never find you."

Fleta stopped struggling. She had to figure a way to survive until Noble and the others came for her. And they would come, she knew.

After discovering his injury was only a badly twisted ankle, Noble limped across to the campfire. Spotted Horse had the pair drag the dead man to the fire. The Osage held the two at gunpoint.

Noble recognized the corpse as Izer Goodman's henchman. "Tennessee Dawson," he whispered. He turned to the other rustlers. "Where's Izer Goodman?" he demanded as he rubbed his aching leg and ankle.

"Who's that?"

Noble took three painful steps and grabbed the youthful rustler, slapping him had. "You better start remembering real quick! Where's Izer?"

"Gone...left us...two days ago."

"Where?"

"Back a ways."

"Get a rope," Noble told Spotted Horse. "We're hanging this pair."

"Wait! We can tell you about Izer, don't hang us!" The other one pleaded.

"You got to promise," he begged, "you won't hang us."

Noble heard his own breath rush in and out of his nose. His arms tense, ready to reach out and strike the quivering pair.

"I promise not to hang you, if what you have to say is worth anything," he relented.

"He's kidnapping your wife," the younger man mumbled.

The words slammed into Noble's gut and he jammed the nose of the Colt in the first man's chest. "This is damn serious. If anything happens to her, I'll scour the earth for the two of you."

"You promised."

"Spotted Horse, can you handle the horses and bring this pair in too?"

"Yes, but you should rest, Noble."

"No, I need that bastard Goodman in my sights." Noble turned back to the rustlers. "Where has he taken her?"

"Honest, Mister, we don't know. He hired us to move some horses. Then Red got mouthy about the guy who owned these horses was going to lose his wife. We wanted to quit, but he said he'd kill us." The rustler turned to his partner. "Wouldn't he have killed us?"

"Yes sir, that's the God's truth."

"Where was he taking her?" Noble stomped his soggy boot, bringing a jarring flash of pain from his ankle.

"He never said."

Damn, Noble swore to himself. Izer Goodman, I'm coming and you'll be sorry if one hair on her head is damaged.

Spotted Horse tightly bound the pair of rustlers. Noble wolfed down some burnt bacon and washed it with two cups of bitter coffee. He was bone tired and only by great effort was he able to sit upright. His eyes were glued on the flames. The heat dried him out but could not warm the cold chills he felt when he thought of Fleta in Izer's grasp.

"Be careful, good friend," the Osage warned as he squatted beside him. "You will recover your woman."

Was that a prophecy like his weather forecasting? Or did the Indian simply want to reassure him. Noble scolded himself for not already being in the saddle and on his way to finding Fleta.

Chapter Thirteen

Sudan was weary and disgusted with his fruitless search for the mired, phantom wagon. He slouched on the wide back of one of the Belgian mares. The harness jingled in cadence with its trot. Rain drummed on Sudan's slicker and ran down his face. He scowled up at the sky. He was on a damned wild goose chase. Why had that crazy man sent him all over Kansas for nothing? Now Noble and Spotted Horse were gone and—

Sudan pulled his thoughts up short. Sweet Jesus! There was no one at the fort guarding the place. Oh hell, if something was wrong at the fort, he'd nail that rascal's hide to the gate.

"Giddiup, mare! We've got a long hard ride ahead of us." Dismayed with his discovery, he worried about how upset and angry Noble would be if anything happened at the fort.

In darkness, he rode through the fort gate. A light in the store window relieved him. Misses was home, thank goodness. There didn't seem to be any signs of trouble.

Yellow Deer burst out of the store and peered into the darkness at him. "Sudan?" she called, leaning from side to side to peer through the thick rain.

"Is everyone all right?" he shouted as he jumped down.

"A man came in a buggy and took Fleta to Noble. The man said Noble was hurt."

Sudan ducked under the porch roof and stood looking down at his woman.

Mannah appeared in the open doorway of the store, the light shining like a halo over her head. "This man was in a big hurry," she said.

"She went—the Misses went with him?" Sudan asked with a puzzled frown.

"Yea," Mannah said. "She sent Luke to get me to close the store."

"How long has she been gone?" Sudan asked, knowing that Indians didn't keep time as the white man did.

Fortunately Luke appeared at the door and answered Sudan's question, "About three hours ago. We better go check on Mama."

"It was all a damned trick," Sudan muttered.

"What's wrong?" Mannah asked.

Sudan waved them inside. "The whole thing was phony. There was no stuck wagon. It was a trick to get me out of the way so those snakes could take her away."

"But why?" Luke asked, his face pale with fear.

The black man turned and was relieved to see Rivers and Barge entering the store carrying their rifles.

"We have been bamboozled by some smart, bad ones," Sudan told them. "Barge, you put up my horse. Rivers, go saddle two fresh horses. We're going to find the Misses tonight. There ain't no injured Noble McCurtain. He might be in a heap of trouble, but he can handle himself all right. It's the Misses we have to find."

"I'll go too," Luke said, starting past him to follow the Indians.

Sudan caught him by the shoulder. "No, sir. Luke, you and Barge got to stay here with the women and hold down the fort. Your daddy has most all he owns in the place. You make Mannah the boss; make sure everyone minds her. You help Barge watch out for trouble. Do you understand, Luke?"

Luke kicked at the floor with his bare toe. "Yes, sir."

Sudan gratefully accepted a cup of tea from one of the women. Where was Yellow Deer? he wondered. She was there a moment ago. He drank the tea in scalding gulps.

Rivers was mounting when Sudan went outside into the rain. Yellow Deer held the reins to Sudan's horse. He walked toward her, his steps weary.

"I'm sorry, woman," he pressed her wet head to his chest and took the reins. He frowned when he noticed the Kiowa buffalo hide shield and lance string tied on the saddle.

"That never helped them Kiowas," he said.

"You take it. Plenty good medicine."

"Girl, I'm going to look strange as hell carrying a Kiowa lance and shield—me not being no Indian."

"Take it for Yellow Deer," she said softly. "It is very good medicine." The look in her eyes convinced him that she was serious.

"All right, I'll take it."

Sudan felt her affectionate slap on his leg before he set out through the dim opening of the gate for the prairie. He knew Rivers would catch up with him in a little while. Praying that he was doing the right thing by leaving the fort to Barge and the women, he tried to clear his thoughts. He had to find the Misses; she meant more to Noble than all the goods in the store. The thing that bothered him most was that the people who tricked him where white men. They were smart, apparently smarter than he was. He had to keep thinking about that while he looked for the Misses.

Rivers dismounted several times and felt around in the darkness for the wet wagon tracks. Although Sudan knew that the Osage couldn't see in the dark either, he trusted the man's instincts.

The Kiowa lance hung under his left leg from a leather strap over the saddle horn. Over his other leg the shield hobbled against him. Sudan shook his head and smiled wryly.

At least the rain was letting up. The horses splashed across a small, storm-swollen creek. Rivers dismounted. Sudan held the reins. The Osage waded back across the stream. Though his eyes searched the inky night, Sudan felt almost blind in the darkness.

Rivers returned, creating big splashes in the water. "Wagon crossed here. Horses over there go east."

"Range horses?"

"No, deep tracks, carrying riders."

"You done good in this cussed night. We better follow the wagon tracks."

When Rivers mounted, they rode south. Perhaps by dawn they'd see the buggy. Sudan wondered about Luke, Barge, and the women. Noble, he said silently, I'm sorry but I'm looking hard for your woman.

In the gray flannel dawn, Sudan spotted the wagon. When they rode up on it, they discovered someone sleeping in the back. The jaded horses in front appeared run near to death. Rivers moved his horse around, studying the ground for tracks.

Sudan poked the sleeper with his carbine barrel. "Wake up, boy!"

"Huh?" The youth's eyes opened and widened with shock at the sight of the huge black man.

"Where is she?" Sudan demanded as he drew his horse nearer the boy.

"Who?"

"Mrs. McCurtain."

"I don't know what you want, nigger."

Sudan cocked the hammer back. "Well you just better get to remembering 'cause I'm having a quake in my trigger finger. Where is she?"

The boy mumbled a name. Sudan couldn't quite make it out, but the boy continued before he could say anything. "There's nothing your black ass can do about it. He'll kill you before you get within ten steps of him."

"Just the same. Where's this Lizard Goldman at?"

"On the Verdigris. You go there and he'll sure kill you."

"How old are you, boy?" Sudan asked.

"Nineteen."

Sudan turned, raised the carbine, and uncocked it. He glanced at Rivers, who was stripping the Kiowa lance off his saddle horn.

Before Sudan could find words to stop him, Rivers drove the Kiowa's spear deep into the wide-eyed boy's chest.

Sudan looked at the youth who was grabbing at the thick shaft, a gurgling sound coming from his mouth. He fell back in the buggy. Feathers fluttered on the shaft as the boy's dying reflexes caused the spear to quiver.

Rivers spat at him. "Son of bitch, good for you to die. Take a good woman away." The Osage said more, but Sudan didn't understand the words. He surmised they had something to do with the boy's life in the hereafter. Perhaps God would forgive the heathen for his actions.

Rivers swung on his horse and left quickly, retracing their back trail.

Sudan spurred his horse after Rivers. Perhaps the Osage knew where the Verde trees were? He might even know this Lizard Goodman.

Slowly the name became familiar. Yes, Sudan recalled, he was the one who had shot Noble's gray horse in Independence. He recalled the stories the Osage told of this Izer Goodman and how he bullied them before Noble came. Whatever that trash had in mind for the Misses was not going to be pleasant. Sudan regretted not retrieving the lance, so he could use it on this Goodman.

Rivers was as glum as Sudan could ever recall him being. His eyes hardly more than slits, his anger seemed to be on the rise.

"You hate that Goodman?"

"Plenty bad. He rob Indians, hurt women."

Sudan decided the Osage was angry enough for the both of them. He looked around, wondering where Noble was.

"How much further, Rivers?"

"Two days ride."

"Hold up," Sudan said. "We'll kill these horses at this rate." But his words fell on deaf ears; Rivers was pushing onward. Sudan drew a resigned breath and booted his horse into a trot. Noble, he said silently, we'll get her back for you. I hope God's riding with you.

Noble, meanwhile, was pushing his stallion northward. He had slept only an hour to rest the gray. His mind was wrought with concern. Had outlaws devastated the fort? A growing dread filled his chest with an emptiness that drained him of strength. His ankle throbbed, swollen tightly inside his leather boot.

Late in the afternoon, he discovered a driverless wagon, the horses grazing in harness. A pole stuck up in the rear box behind the spring seat. Pistol in his hand, he rode closer.

"Damn," Noble swore aloud. "They killed him with a spear." The bloated dead man was a stranger. What tribe had done this to him?

He dismounted heavily and, with wooden movements, unhitched the team, turning them loose. He had had no sleep in forty-eight hours and knew his lack of rest was catching up with him. Wearily, he crawled up in the saddle again with only a passing regret for the dead man. No time to bury the stranger; he had to push on.

His mind was numb and even the sight of the fort still intact did not generate any great emotion within him. The tired gray stallion grunted with tiredness to match his own exhaustion.

"Noble!" Luke shouted, bursting through the store door. "They took mama away to find you."

"What? Who did?" he asked, unable to comprehend what the boy was telling him. Total exhaustion blanketed his brain with cotton wool. Thinking was too much of an effort. He dismounted, dragged his aching leg toward the porch and his eyes narrowed with puzzlement as he stared down at Luke.

"Sudan and Rivers went to find Mama. Some man in a buckboard came here and told her you were hurt."

"How long ago?" Noble asked.

"Two days."

For a long moment, Noble tried to sort out the situation. It was no use; he had to get some sleep. His eyes burned like fire and his eyelids were lead-weighted. His actions were those of a drunk man as he pulled himself up the steps of the store. Too tired to fully comprehend his loss, he fought to stay awake.

"Wake me up in four hours," he mumbled.

He shook his head at Mannah's offer of food. Staggering back to the bedroom, he tried to block out all his fears for Fleta. Filled with guilt at his own inability to go further, he sprawled face down on the quilt cover and was asleep within minutes.

Izer appeared to be in a big hurry to reach his place—wherever that might be. Fleta's entire body was sore. Her ribs ached from being in a belly-down position on Izer's saddle. She was grateful for the horse the outlaws had finally procured for her.

She was still aghast by the earlier actions of the scar-faced boy called Yank. When they had stopped a few hours earlier, Izer had rode off to check their back trail.

Yank grabbed her without warning. His rotten breath nearly

gagged her and his stubbled beard scraped her face raw when he tried to kiss her. Then Izer rode up and savagely slashed Yank on the side of the head with his pistol barrel. Yank released her at once and slumped to his knees, holding his head.

Fleta was stunned at the senseless brutality. Yank, with blood running over his ear, cursed Izer loudly.

"She's mine!" Izer growled. "I told you twice. Next time, I'll blow your guts out."

Izer walked over to her, holstering his gun. He grabbed her by the arm and jerked her roughly up against his chest. "You're mine, woman. Just so you know, I'm going to blow that damned Noble's head off when he rides in after you."

His sour body odor burned her nose. Fleta forced down a wave of revulsion that rose in her throat. His rough hands pawed at her breasts, knifing her with pain, but she tightened her jaw muscles in defiance, determined not to show any fear.

He laughed and pulled her closer. "Keep thinking, gal. I know you are, but he ain't going to save you. 'Cause I'm gonna kill him!"

His fingers gouged her upper arm, creating deep purple bruises on her skin. Izer shoved her away, causing her to stumble a few steps. One thought dominated her mind and kept her from giving up: Noble would kill this filthy Izer Goodman.

After two days with the outlaws, she began to notice small things, like how Izer kept looking nervously at their back trail. She'd seen him flinch at the least sound. Once a fox squirrel on a post oak limb startled him so much he nearly fell off his horse. Izer didn't fool her; he *was* worried about Noble finding them.

She detected a slight change in the men in the afternoon. They seemed more familiar with the country they crossed. Struck with the notion they must be near Izer's cabin, her heart beat faster. She needed to form a plan and time was running out.

Sudan knew, without dismounting to check, the horse droppings were fresh. He saw the excitement on River's face. He also knew the Osage wanted revenge like nothing else ever before.

"They were here," the Osage said. "Not long ago." He squatted and seemed to study something, then he waved Sudan over.

"What is it?" Sudan asked slipping off his horse.

"Blood."

"I'll be damned. I sure hope it ain't the Misses." As much as he wanted to hurry, he decided their weary horses needed a respite. If them scruffy bastards hurt her, they would sure pay. His travel-muddled mind could not conceive a punishment severe enough to inflict on the kidnappers.

"They go to Izer's cabin," Rivers said.

"Yeah, guess these poor horses can rest when we find her," Sudan shook his head as he remounted.

Fleta trembled inside. Her eyes searched the brown leafed pot oaks that surrounded the hideout. Where was Noble? Why hadn't he come?

"Get down," Izer ordered her. "Brown Boy. Put these horses in the pen. What's the matter with you?" he asked Yank.

"Gawd damn you, Izer, you broke my damn skull. I got a headache that—"

"Shut up, or I'll make it worse," Izer said, as he shoved Fleta ahead of him toward the front door of the shack.

Inside, the dank interior struck her forcibly in the face. It stunk of old hides and the rank odor of urine. Her optimism began to sink. The cabin's tomb-like atmosphere cut off her hopes. The outline of Yank in the doorway against the low cast sun was like a nail sealing her doom.

"Yank," Izer said. "You touch her before I get back, I'll blow your stupid head off."

Fleta noticed Izer seemed to be checking crock jugs for something to drink. His search apparently was futile. He whirled around to scowl at Yank again.

"Did you hear me?"

"Yeah! She'll be here."

"Listen to me! That headache will be the least of your troubles if you mess with her."

"All right!" Yank gingerly held his hand to the side of his head.

"I'm going after some whiskey," Izer said. "Make sure she stays here. If Dawson ain't killed her husband, I figure a bunch of them blanket-ass Osage will be coming around. Just shoot them. You listening to me?''

"My damned head hurts," Yank whined, but made sure Izer was not close enough to hit him again.

Izer's face blackened with rage. The lines along his cheeks were deep; his beaky nose quivered with rage. "You better do what I've told you!"

"Okay, okay. We'll watch for them."

The Indian walked inside looking mildly from Izer to Yank.

"You better listen! I want this place guarded while I'm gone," Izer directed his words to Brown Boy. "Don't mess with her either!"

Fleta saw the Indian nod. How much time would she have with the boys before Izer came back? She needed to outsmart them. The drumming hooves of Goodman's horse faded.

She was in such deep thought that Yank's first words startled her.

"Light a lamp," he ordered her sharply.

"No matches," she said through tight lips.

Yank grumbled and drew back his hand as if to slap her. Then he moved off to pilfer in a trunk. Returning, he snapped a sulfurous match and laughed as she flinched.

Fleta drew a deep breath. The stupid outlaw with dried blood on his greasy straight hair would be no threat to a man. She watched him light a candle stub and spit on the waning match.

"Now fix us some food."

"What is there to fix?" she asked with a shrug.

"Hell, I don't know. But get busy looking for something," Yank snarled as if he wanted to vent some of his pent up anger against her.

Fleta found some unwashed kettles. She wrinkled her nose in disgust at the dried food crusted inside them. "I'll need some water to wash these."

"Scrape them. Brown Boy will be back in a minute; he can go get some water."

With a wooden spoon, she began cleaning the kettles. She looked around for a knife or something sharp to pry away the stale food.

"Boy!" Yank shouted. "Bring some water in here." Out of

breath, Yank coughed so deeply that he bent over double. "Son of a bitch." Gasping for breath, he spread his hands on the table to support himself.

Fleta considered rushing out the door but she would probably only run into the silent Boy. Besides, she had no weapon, no way to disable a man. The thought caused her to renew her search for something sharp. She found nothing but cornmeal crawling with worms. She closed the sack quickly and stifled a gagging cough of her own.

"You find anything to eat?" Yank wheezed at her.

"There's nothing here," she retorted, kicking a broken crate out of her path. She scowled in disgust at the filthy cabin, then placed her hands on her hips and glared at Yank.

Brown Boy came inside with a bucket of water. He set it on the crooked table and looked at Yank, whose face was still red from his coughing spell. "What's wrong?"

"She can't find a gawdamned thing to cook." He pointed at her accusingly. "Damnit, I say Izer left us to starve with her. You hear me, Brown Boy?"

Fleta felt the Indian's eyes on her but she did not look at him.

"Now, Izer ain't paid us. All he's fed us so far is some stale crackers and jerky. Hell, it's been a damned week now since we had a decent meal. I say we use her, take his horses, and get the hell out of here."

Yank's suggestion sounded crazy, but Boy's dark eyes had an equally unsettling effect on Fleta. Who else but madmen would work for Izer Goodman?

"He won't be back for hours," Yank coaxed Boy. "Might be gone a day if his whiskey man's gone or out of whiskey."

"He'll be mad," Boy said uncertainly.

"Who cares?"

Boy laughed. "Izer will be damned mad." A new sound, like a clucking in Boy's throat, filled Fleta with apprehension. It was not the laugh of a normal sane person. The sands in her hourglass were running out quickly.

Yank started around her one way, Brown Boy advanced on the other side. Stepping backward, Fleta nearly tumbled over the broken crate. A bed was behind her—something she wanted to be well away from. She looked from one man to the other, frantically trying to decide which one to go for. With a cry of desperation, Fleta charged, her elbows pointed outward in defense. Yank went down, but she almost fell on top of him.

"Grab her!" Yank shouted. "Get the bitch!"

She nearly made it to the door, but Brown Boy's thick red arms halted her. He held her hands behind her back and marched her toward Yank. She tried to duck the stinging blow that Yank aimed at her, but his hand connected with the side of her head.

Yank tore at her clothes. The material ripped and separated as she struggled in Boy's grasp. His hands fondled her exposed breasts. She groaned and writhed, trying to avoid his filthy touch.

Yank began unfastening his britches. Boy dragged her back toward the bed. Her screaming fell empty on the dank air as she was pinned to the rough blankets. Fleta tried to bite at the men as the last ribbons of her undergarments were torn from her body. With her legs flailing the air and her long auburn hair flying about her face, she shouted obscenities at her molesters. Her words and actions had no effect on the two panting men.

Yank maneuvered himself between her legs. Fleta screamed and braced herself for the inevitable. She squeezed her eyes tightly and tried to bring her knees together, but Boy held them apart.

A wild scream of rage erupted in the room. Brown Boy released her and turned. Yank tried to pull up his britches. Fleta drew the blanket up to cover her nakedness. Her eyes were blinded with tears; she could not see who the newcomer was. Then the man screamed in outrage again and she recognized Rivers.

The Osage was on Brown Boy, slashing and stabbing him with a large knife. The Indian was completely out of control, his rage making him deaf to anyone's pleas.

Sudan was beating on the whining Yank with a large club. Blow after blow thudded on the outlaw, the thunking sound weighing heavily on the air.

A gurgling caused Fleta to glance at Rivers. Her eyes rounded with horror and nausea clawed at her insides. She jerked her head away. Rivers was decapitating Brown Boy. She wanted all this madness to stop but was unable to speak. Covering her head with the blanket, she put her hands over both ears to drown out the sounds of the two dying men. When her mind seemed ready to snap, Fleta fainted.

It seemed only moments later that she was wrapped in a blanket and being carried away by Sudan.

"We had to get out quick, Misses. The cabin's on fire. Me and Rivers, we ain't looking on you none, ma'am. We'll find you some clothes. But the damned fire's going to warn Izer and I sure wanted to get him."

Fleta made an attempt to cover more of herself with the blanket. When she looked up at Sudan, tears were streaming down his purplish-black cheeks.

"You did fine, Sudan," she whispered. "Thank you."

Sudan could not control his tears. The weight of the Misses seemed like nothing. The cabin crackled behind them. He thought that death was not enough punishment for the two men who had harmed Noble's wife. Even now, he wanted his hands back on them, punishing them.

"Sudan," Fleta said softly, "I can walk."

Gently he placed her on the ground, steadying her with his big hands. Then he went to his saddle and removed the canvas coat lashed behind it. He shook it and held it out to Fleta, his eyes downcast.

Gratefully Fleta shrugged off the odious blanket and slipped into Sudan's roomy canvas coat. Her fingers fumbled with the buttons and she noted that Sudan tactfully looked away until she was decently clothed. She rolled up the overly long sleeves and pushed them up to her elbows.

"Where did Rivers go?" she asked.

"He's looking for Izer. We couldn't find him."

"He went after some whiskey when we got here."

"Rivers sure wants him bad. I figure he'll stay on his trail 'til he finds him."

"Where's Noble?" she asked, peering anxiously up into his face.

Sudan shook his head. "He wasn't back yet when we left."

"Oh no!" Fleta wailed, wringing her hands with worry. What if something bad had happened to him? What if he had really been injured?

"Now, Misses," Sudan patted her shoulder awkwardly. "Don't worry about Noble McCurtain. He's just fine. I know he is."

"Sudan," she said, pausing for a deep breath. "I never even thanked you and Rivers properly."

"Ain't no need to, ma'am. I have some food for you," he said hurriedly to cover up his embarrassment at her words.

"I—I'm not hungry." Totally exhausted, Fleta eased herself down on the ground. The cabin was now a crackling inferno in the night. Yank and Brown Boy's bodies were being cremated. She turned away from the sight.

"Is Rivers coming back?" she asked.

"No, Misses," Sudan said quietly. He looked at her sharply, wondering if she was all right. Although he already told her where the Indian was, he repeated it again, "He's gone to find Izer Goodman."

"Doesn't Rivers need your help?"

"No, ma'am. I'm going to round up a horse and get you home to Noble quick as I can."

"But—"

Sudan shook his head and held up a hand. "Don't you worry none about Rivers. He be all right." Although Sudan wanted to follow Rivers and catch up with Izer, he knew he had to get the Misses home quickly. Besides, he thought, Rivers was a good man; he could take care of himself. The Osage would handle that damned Izer snake.

Fleta felt very uncomfortable in the stiff voluminous coat, also very conscious of being naked beneath it as she rode behind Sudan on one of the extra horses. Her head pounded and felt sore where Yank had slapped her. Bruises covered her arms and legs and she dreaded to think what Noble would do when he saw them. If he saw them. Oh where could he be? she fretted. She clutched at the saddle horn to keep from falling. Her head swam and she had to make a determined effort not to faint again.

"Are you all right, Misses?" Sudan asked over his shoulder. The trail through the post oaks meandered uphill and was not an easy route. He wondered if he were going too fast for the Misses.

"I'm fine," she lied to no avail. Darkness engulfed her and she felt herself falling sideways, but she did not have the strength to save herself.

When she opened her eyes, it took her a moment to sort out what had happened. Apparently Sudan had laid her on a bedroll and covered her up with his blanket. He sat across from her, his knees drawn up, the Winchester across his lap. His brown eyes studied the hills in the distance. Sun bathed the brown world about to sprout green. A hint of elm leaves, like a promise of things to come, was present.

Fleta lay immobile, looking at the scenery. The land was like Arkansas. The hills were shorter. Wilbourne would be plowing now. Why was she thinking of him? she wondered. She was on her way home to Noble McCurtain.

"Morning, Misses," Sudan said quietly. "Are you feeling better?"

She struggled to rise to a sitting position. "Yes, I think so. I guess I was tired."

"Yes, ma'am. I should have waited, but I knowed you was anxious to get away from that place."

"Yes, I was. Thanks."

"I got some water from a clear little spring that's pure as honey," he offered persuasively.

"Good. I'm very thirsty." It took a great deal of effort for her to remain sitting up, but she managed.

"Ain't nothing hurting you, is there?"

"No, just my pride," she said with a strained smile.

"Mercy sakes, you did take a nasty spill off that horse when you fainted."

"Well, I'm just fine."

"Eat some crackers." He held out some soda crackers on his palm. "It's all I got," he said apologized.

"I think I could manage one or two of those," she said.

By mid-day they were on the move again. Fleta realized the trail they were traveling led to the top of a mountain. She'd been so wrought up on the way to Goodman's place, that she knew she'd never have managed to find the way back alone. Marveling at the beautiful panorama in all directions, her spirits lifted a little. Sudan's hand on her arm broke the spell.

"Ain't that Mr. Noble's hat?" he asked, pointing at a distant rider.

She squinted. Yes, it looked like his gray Stetson. The rider *was* Noble. Her heart pounded with anticipation. Without a thought, she gave her horse its head and raced westward on the trail through the gray broom sedge. It was Noble and, thank God, he was alive!

Moments later they were both off their horses and racing toward each other with arms outstretched. Noble lifted her high in the air and swung her around. He buried his face in her hair, holding her so tightly her sore ribs ached in protest. But she said nothing of her pain; it was an exquisite pain.

"My God, Fleta, are you all right?"

"I—I'm fine, Noble," she said breathlessly. "I was so worried about you." She leaned back in his arms to get a good look at his dear face.

"I'm all right now." He squeezed her again.

Noble saw the horses and looked up into the serious brown eyes above him. Sudan was holding the horses and obviously he had something on his mind.

"What is it, Sudan?"

"Now that the Misses is safely with you, I want your permission to go find Rivers. Me and him got a bone to pick with Izer Goodman."

Noble considered the request. He wanted Izer for himself, to blow his grizzly face off this earth. "Sudan, you're a free man. You don't need my permission. No one can tell you what to do. Go with by blessings."

"Mister Noble?"

"Just Noble," he corrected the black man.

"Noble, you look after Yellow Deer for me. Ain't no telling where Rivers has gone to find Goodman."

"Wait, you'll need some money." Noble released Fleta and shoved his hands down in his pockets. "All I have is a few dollars." He handed the money over to Sudan.

"Thank you." Sudan nodded to both of them.

"No, I'm grateful to you," Noble said, his arm over Fleta's shoulders protectively. "Be careful, my friend."

"Winchester and me. We will." Then he swung his horse around and rode back in the direction of Izer's cabin.

"Will he be all right?" Fleta asked worriedly.

"Yes." Noble watched the man ride away. "Yes, he can take care of himself."

They stood in silence, worn by relief. Noble swept Fleta into his arms. "We need to get home. We've got two days ride ahead of us."

"Can we hurry?"

"Yes." He set her on her horse, surprised at his own strength. He cast a last glance toward the trail that Sudan had taken, but the black man was gone. "Let's go home, Fleta."

Chapter Fourteen

Sudan was in a strange land—Arkansas. Not since he had been a free man in Alabama had he been among so many settlers. He felt conspicuous in his buckskins. The people eyed him suspiciously.

The trail that Rivers left was so dim he couldn't possibly follow it. Instead, he simply asked people if someone fitting Izer's description had passed by.

"He's a frontier man," Sudan described Izer to one settler, "wears buckskin, has a beard and a wide brim, flat crowned hat made of rawhide." He had learned that much about Goodman from Rivers.

The farmer spat a brown stream of tobacco on the ground between his shoes. "May have passed here. What you need with him?"

"He kidnapped a white lady. My boss' wife, sir." Sudan knew white folks liked polite blacks.

"White woman, huh?"

"This Izer Goodman is a bad man," Sudan said.

"That new rifle belong to you, boy?" The farmer jerked a thumb toward the gun.

"Yes sir. My boss, Noble McCurtain, give me this here rifle."

"Noble McCurtain? Never heard of him."

"He lives in Kansas."

The man spat again and shook his grizzly head. "Never been

there. This man you described rode by here—ah—about two days ago. Course, it could have been..." He paused and rubbed his bristly jaw. "When did it last rain? I figured he was going to Cincinnati, Arkansas. There'a lots of his kind that go there."

"How far is that, sir?" Sudan asked, trying to stem his impatience at the man's slow speech.

"Down the road a piece. You can't miss it. Sodom and Gomorrah. Full of saloons. No place for God-fearing people."

"Yes, sir. I appreciate the information."

"You a free slave?" The man peered up at Sudan with curiosity.

"Yes sir. Mr. Lincoln set us all free."

"Guess he did at that." The farmer scratched a thatch of hair over his right ear. "I could use a strong man like you around here."

Sudan looked down at his dusty boot toes. "Thank you, but when I finish my business with this Izer Goodman, I have me a job already. Up in Kansas with Mr. McCurtain."

"Probably ought to go back there then. They won't treat you too good in Cincinnati. Not with you being a nigger and all."

"I'll remember that," Sudan said, leaping back on his horse.

Cincinnati, Arkansas was a series of buildings astraddle the main road. A mill was situated on the creek; four saloons, two hotels, a post office, and a school house completed the town. Sudan circled around carefully. That farmer's parting words had been meant as a warning, and he intended to be ready for the people of Cincinnati. He had now crossed into the south—the land of slave owners. And Mr. Lincoln was dead. There was no telling how these southerners would treat a wandering black man.

A young black woman emerged from the rear of one of the hotels. He rode up beside her.

"Ma'am," he said quietly, "I'm a stranger here. I need some information."

She stared up in disbelief when Sudan stepped down off his horse and nodded politely. "Why'd you go scaring me like that?" She wrapped her shawl around her shoulders and flung her head back angrily.

"You work in that hotel?"

"Well, you sure can't get a room there," she said, her eyes mocking. "They don't allow no niggers in there."

"My name's Sudan Wilson."

Her wide nostrils flares and she appraised him with a look of contempt. "Well, Mr. Sudan Wilson, just because you's dressed up like some Injun, don't make you white."

Sudan's lips clamped tight to control his anger. "I don't give a damn about no hotel room," he said coldly. "I want to know whether a certain man's been there or not."

"Who?"

"Name's Izer Goodman. Wears buckskin, big bushy beard, long dirty hair."

She was silent for a moment, then nodded her head. "He's gone on. An Injun what got put in jail was looking for him too."

"What you saying, girl?" Sudan reached out a hand as if to grab her, then let it drop to his side. "What Indian?"

The woman sighed heavily then pulled at the bright kerchief around her head. "Some fool Injun went into the saloon with a rifle. Well, he sure be a crazy one. He asked for this Izer man and someone hit him over the head. He whipped four or five big white men after he was hit. A real crazy Injun."

"Damn Rivers," Sudan muttered beneath his breath. He looked around. "Where's the jail?"

"Up the hill, see there." The woman pointed toward a log shed at the top of the steep street. "They sent word for the Injun police to come and get him."

"Why?"

She clucked her teeth and twitched her shawl tighter, "Cause the man be crazy."

"What kind of Indian police?"

"Lordy sake, man. You think I got nothing better to do than stand here and answer your fool questions all day? I's got work to do."

"I'm sorry, ma'am, but I need to know what kind of police," Sudan growled.

"Cherokee."

"Who's got the key to the jail?"

Her brown eyes rounded and she took a step backward, "Why, the constable, but—"

"When this Izer Goodman leave town?" Sudan cut in abruptly.

"Days ago."

"Where'd he go?"

"Fort Smith, I guess. That road goes there. But don't you be thinking about getting that Injun out of jail. They'll just lock you up beside him."

"What's your name?" Sudan asked with a grin.

She sniffed and turned her shoulder. "Opie. But I's already got me a man."

Sudan shook his head. "Well, Opie, I've got myself a woman too. You go out there and see that if that constable be watching."

"He ain't watching. He's playing cards in the hotel. What you gonna do, Sudan Wilson?" She asked with a frown of disapproval.

"Don't worry your pretty head, girl. You just get on about your business."

"Black man, if you do what I think you're planning, you'd best get done and ride west fast."

"Why?"

"That's just a litle way to Injun land. Constable can't go there."

When Sudan digested this piece of information, he smiled in gratitude. "Well, Miss Opie, you are one fine lady."

"You're a man of class yourself, Sudan Wilson. That constable won't miss that crazy Injun, but he'll sure be mad as hell if you bust the lock on his jail."

Sudan watched her swaying hips as she sauntered away, whistling to herself. He admired her for a moment. There sure weren't any Indian women looked like that walking away from you.

He rode his horse up the rutted road, guiding the gelding to the log shed under some giant oaks. With a sense of relief, he noticed the town seemed practically deserted at this hour of the day. From the protection of the trees, he moved the horse toward the iron grated doors.

"Rivers," he hissed through the opening. "You in there?"

"Huh? Sudan, is that you?" a haggard sounding Rivers whispered back.

"Get back, I'm going to shoot that lock."

"Good," the Osage grunted.

The black man took aim. The rifle boomed; his horse shied and the powder smoke boiled. "Come on, crazy Osage!" Sudan wheeled his mount. Five or six men had run out of the saloons down the hill.

Rivers ran outside, waving aside the gunsmoke. He stepped into the stirrup and swung up behind Sudan. Sensing the tension, the horse responded and took off in a gallop. Below the hill, the men began shouting for the constable.

Since the horse was headed west, Sudan let him run.

"Izer got my rifle," Rivers grumbled behind him. "Now I kill the son-of-a-bitch with a knife."

"Hell, he's gone to Fort Smith," Sudan said, holding him aside so he could see if they were being pursued. "We better get back to Noble. We'll get Izer later."

"No! I go to Fort Smith. Kill him there."

"Damnit, you crazy Injun. We're wanted men in Arkansas now for jail breaking." Sudan shook his head in exasperation as the Osage grumbled in his ear. The wild goose chase was over for now. Izer Goodman was gone again. Noble would not be pleased to hear the news. They had lost a good repeater too. And the law would probably never know how the Osage got busted out of jail. Hell, they were just lucky to be on their way back home.

In Kansas, Fleta continued to experience shaky spells from her ordeal at the hands of Izer's thugs. She assured Noble she was getting better, but still he worried.

"Noble," she told him one evening after he had again expressed his concern, "I only have these spells when I'm tired. They're less frequent now."

"We have too much business," he said with a shake of his head. "We're busier this year than we were last year. I'll hire you some help."

"Oh, I'll be fine." She smiled weakly and squeezed his hand, wanting to erase the lines of worry etched on his forehead. Why was she so weak? The memory of Yank and the Boy's hands on her skin and of their subsequent deaths lingered in her mind and caused her to tremble. She simply couldn't forget.

"Someone's in the store," he said, upon hearing the jingle of the bell affixed to the door. "I'll go wait on them."

"I was just fixing to put dinner on the table. Hurry back."

"Don't worry about my supper. You just sit by the fire and rest." He walked toward the store area and smiled at the broad man standing at the counter. "Could I help you?"

"Are you Noble McCurtain?"

"Yes."

"My name's Fortney Lincolnshire. My wife and children are back a ways. Our wagon broke down and I came to see if you could help."

"Certainly. My blacksmith's gone, but I'll send Spotted Horse back with you and you can come up here for the night. Tomorrow, I'll go help you get your wagon here."

The man frowned and paused uncertainly. "Who's this Spotted Horse?"

"A man who works for me," Noble said with a raised brow, wondering at the man's unfriendly attitude.

"He an Injun?"

"Osage. But I guarantee he won't scalp you." Noble's attempt at humor was met with a scowl of distaste.

"Nope. I'll have no diseased buck around my wife or family."

"Diseased?" Noble frowned at the man.

"They all got diseases. I know all about it. No thanks, McCurtain!" The man turned toward the door.

"Mr. Lincolnshire? My misses is not well or I'd go with you. But you may hitch up my team of Belgians and take the wagon out there. Spotted Horse would sure help you, but I'd say if you're dead set against it, you can go hitch it up yourself."

"I'm obliged to you." The man touched the brim of his floppy hat.

Noble shook his head in wonder at the man's retreating back. He walked back in the living area, a puzzled look on his face.

"Who was it?" Fleta asked from her position in the rocker.

"A man with a broken down wagon, who seems to think that Indians are diseased. I loaned him our team and wagon."

"Diseased?"

Noble moved toward the stove where his supper was kept warming. "He had some crazy notion about Indians. I offered to send Spotted Horse to help him bring his family in here, but he refused my offer."

Fleta set the rocker in gentle motion. "He may steal Sudan's mares."

"No, I don't think the man is a thief," Noble said, taking down his plate of food. "He's a broken down settler."

Fleta sighed softly. "Eat your supper. I swear, Noble, I believe that you'd help the devil himself if he asked you to."

"Aw, Fleta, you remember how hard things were for you. Well, I was so hungry when I first left home that if farmers hadn't fed me, I would have starved to death. It was tough when I left my uncle's place and struck out on my own.

"One night near St. Louis, a black man shared his soup with me. Had boiled turnip greens and some stuff I didn't recognize. I think it might have been possum. I hadn't eaten in two days. The man never said, 'You're white, go on and get out of here.' He said, 'Sit down and eat.' "

Fleta smiled. There was so much she did not know about her man. To pry was not her way, although she was curious. She savored Noble's reflections when he shared them with her.

"You better get some rest. I'll wait up to see if this settler gets back."

"Noble, I'll be all right. You can stop worrying about me."

Fleta did not go directly to bed. She stayed up, afraid to sleep lest she have dreams about Izer and his two massacred companions.

Noble felt restless as well. He took a walk around the settlement, noting the compound was becoming crowded with tepees. Soon, he would have to ask the Osage to move outside the fort so there'd be enough room. He knew they felt welcome and secure, surely they wouldn't mind moving a few yards away.

"Noble!" Spotted Horse called out to him.

When Noble reached the chief standing near the gates, he saw the Osage shaking his head. "Strange man who took the wagon."

"He fears Indians," Noble explained. "He should have stayed back east."

"Strange man." The Osage nodded that he understood Noble. "The wind will blow up rain."

"Good." Noble never doubted his forecasts. "That will keep down the danger of a fire before the prairie is green."

Noble watched the Osage's silent retreat. He had grown accustomed to the Indian's abrupt manner. But he never doubted the vigil the Osage kept on the fort, or their loyalty.

He walked out to study the star-studded sky. Soon spring would begin to make itself known. The buffalo would come back. The v's of geese were already heading north.

Where were Sudan and Rivers? They were long overdue. Had they caught up with Izer? Perhaps they'd killed the black hearted outlaw. God, he wished they'd show up soon! Oh well, might as well go back and try to get some sleep.

Sudan and Rivers were in the Indian Territory at a place called Seegar's Store. Seegar was a white man who sold store goods out of a log cabin. A short, wide man waddled out to the corral to meet Sudan and Rivers.

"I got some good horses to sell." Seegar rocked on his heels and looked from one man to the other.

Sudan eyed the winter-thin, mud-caked ponies in the pen. "I'll give you ten dollars for two of them," he said flatly.

"And leave me that cripple you two rode in on? No, sir. Do you take me for a fool?" The man's face flushed almost purple with indignation.

Sudan did not answer. He stiffened warily when two strangers rode past them. He did not miss the hostile look they gave him and Rivers. One of the riders was tall, the other short. Sudan thought they might have been Indians, although they wore store-bought clothes.

"You look at them horses good," Seegar said. "I'll see what those two want." He waddled over to the other men who waited in front of the store.

Rivers looked at the horses again and shook his head in disapproval. "Not worth much."

"Not unless you got money," Sudan agreed.

"We can't afford Seegar's horses. Guess I'm a dang fool, I

forget how much things cost."

"No money," Rivers said as if he completely understood their financial situation.

The strangers went into the store with the chubby storekeeper. Sudan listened as an argument erupted inside. Seegar's voice had a high-pitched whine.

The black man cautiously slid the Winchester out of the scabbard. Trouble was about to break loose in the cabin, he could tell by the tone of the loud voices.

The taller man rushed outside, looked around wildly then fired his pistol point blank at Sudan. The shot went wild. Without a second thought, Sudan raised the Winchester in one hand. His bullet sent the man staggering back against the side of the store. A roar of a shotgun blast sounded and the shorter man backed out clutching his stomach, gut shot. His weaving form stumbled then tumbled off the porch.

Nosing the double barrel ahead of him, Seegar came into view. He raised his gun and shot the short man again as he lay below the porch.

"Sons of bitches were going to rob me!" he shouted.

He looked at Sudan with a frown. "If you bury those two, I'll give you two horses."

Sudan was afraid to ask if the man he had shot was dead. He just nodded.

"Well," Seegar said impatiently. "Go get a shovel, they're around back." He scowled down at the bloody corpses. "Sons of bitches should have known better."

Sudan exchanged a look of disgust with Rivers. "Mr. Seegar, where do you want these two buried?"

"Out there," he waved his hand and pointed toward some mounds beyond the corral, "with the rest of them."

Sudan raised a brow. "Where they robbers too, sir?"

"Hell, this is tough country, boy. Real tough." His voice held a warning. "One hole's enough for both of them."

Sudan dug most of the single grave. Seegar rolled the bigger man off the porch. Rivers used a pick to bust the rocks that delayed their digging. Neither he nor Sudan had much to say.

"That's some tough fat man," Sudan grunted finally. "Wonder

if Izer comes here? Maybe we could get Seegar to send word to us if Izer comes," he said thoughtfully. He spaded the ground wondering if two sorry horses were worth all this bother.

Seegar brought them some crackers and a jug of liquor.

"You hungry?"

"We sure are," Sudan said, "but me and the Osage don't drink."

"It's good lightning—corn made," Seegar said persuasively.

"Thanks anyway." Sudan took some crackers and sat on the ground to eat them. Rivers' face was carved in a granite scowl. Sudan smothered a laugh, knowing that Rivers considered grave digging to be a woman's work.

"That's deep enough," Seegar said a little later. "I could use some men like you two. This is tough country," he slurred the words after taking a big swig of the lightning.

"Mr. Seegar, you mind if me and Rivers take our horses now? Noble McCurtain will be worried that we ain't back yet."

Seegar laughed. "He must be a worrier. Why, you two could sure make your way home."

"How many times have you been robbed?" Sudan asked curiously.

"Never been robbed. Been tried three or four times though."

"They all got killed trying, huh?"

"Sure."

Sudan pursed his lips, then spoke off-handedly, "Mr. Seegar, Izer Goodman ever come here?"

"No!" Seegar's answer was so quick and forceful Sudan was immediately suspicious.

"Did he ever try to rob you?"

"No." Seegar looked away.

"He did something to you?" Sudan persisted.

Seegar kicked up some dirt and took another drink of lightning. He wiped his mouth on his sleeve and muttered bitterly, "He killed my woman."

When Seegar turned away, Sudan thought he might be crying. He motioned to Rivers. The Osage nodded and the two went to catch the two horses. Rivers slipped on his horse bareback with a rope bridle while Sudan switched his saddle and bridle to the new one. The horses were not strong but Sudan knew they would carry them a long ways toward home. He longed to share Yellow Deer's bed of soft skins. A man belonged with his woman.

Chapter Fifteen

At sunup, Noble stood in the doorway, sipping tea and watching the Lincolnshire family dismount from the wagon in a sleepy daze. Two teenage girls, a young boy, and a small girl stood obediently beside the wagon. Noble wondered where the man's wife was.

Fortney stomped across the yard, his expression sullen. "I'll not camp in here with them savages, Mr. McCurtain," he said, pointing to the Osages.

Noble shrugged. "Then camp wherever you like. You may use my wagon until yours is fixed."

Fortney nodded curtly, then gave his family abrupt orders to climb back inside the wagon.

"Where's his wife?" Fleta asked from behind Noble.

"I never saw her. She may be lying down. He sure is headed in the wrong direction if he hates Indians so bad."

"Are you going to help him?"

"Yeah, I reckon so." Noble ushered her back toward the house section of the store. "I just wish Sudan and Rivers would get back."

"Noble," she said impatiently, "will you listen to me?"

Noble paused, his brows raised in mild surprise. "Certainly, Fleta."

"That man out there," she jerked her head towards the window, "is trouble. I'm not sure why, but I just know he's going to be trouble."

"I'll handle it."

Fortney and the young boy brought his wheel into the fort. After inspecting the roped-on rim lumped over the corded tread, Noble rose to his feet. "The rim will have to be shrunk. My blacksmith will be back in a few days."

"A few days! Just when is that, Mr. McCurtain?" Fortney asked with his perpetual scowl.

Noble looked at the embittered man through narrowed eyes. "I can't say exactly. I can tell you is that he's due back anytime."

Fortney frowned but finally shrugged and walked away toward the gate. The boy, who was close to Luke's age, hurried after his father.

Noble watched them leave, wondering about Fleta's warning. It was hard to be courteous to a man so curt. As soon as Sudan returned, he'd fix the wheel and Fortney could move on west.

That afternoon Noble was reminded by the silent cold forge that his blacksmith and Rivers were still absent. Sudan had been gone too long. Surely nothing had happened to him and Rivers on their search for Izer Goodman. The name caused a raw feeling of pain in Noble's gut—Izer Goodman was all that kept him from living in peace.

Noble saddled a bay horse to ride out and check on the Texas cows that were calving. He would keep his distance, for the long-horned parents were poised to hook or butt anyone or anything who disturbed their newborns.

Fortney's bunch attached a canvas shade to their wagon. A smoky fire of buffalo chips was being attended to by the teenage girls.

"Good afternoon," Noble said as he rode up. "Is your father here?"

Uncertainty veiled the girls' faces as they exchanged a look. The fair haired one squinted up at him. "No. He's not my father, but my man. He's gone to get our oxen and stock."

"Oh!" Noble exclaimed, taken aback by her frank words. Why, the girl looked little more than fourteen. "You're Mrs. Lincolnshire?"

"Yes," she said, her red-rimmed eyes narrowing in the sun as she continued to stare up at him.

"My wife's name is Fleta. She would probably enjoy a visit. If you have time, please go up to the store and see her."

She shook her head. "My man said to stay out of there."

"Yes Ma'am." Noble touched his hat in farewell, then wheeled his horse. My lord, Noble thought, she's hardly more than a child and married already. She might not be a suitable wife, but then he figured that Lincolnshire was no bargain either.

As Noble rode, he noted that springtime was coming. The yellow breasted meadowlark exclaimed it everywhere. The grayish tan mat of grass was about to emerge into a carpet of green. Shaggy coated horses lifted their heads to follow him with their eyes. He knew their winter wool must be itching them. Even now the long hair peeled off their jaws and the inside of their legs.

His trading and purchases had increased the horse herd to nearly fifty. Several mares had swollen bellies, thanks to Colonel Custer's gift, the gray stallion. Satisfied that the bulk of his horses were present, Noble rode on to check the scattered groups of cattle.

Spindly newborn calves jumped at his approach and raced deer-like to their mommas. Momma would shake her head rack, but when he rode no closer, she would return to grazing. His cattle herd was growing. Though the store supported Noble and his family, he enjoyed his prospering cattle operation.

Another wagon train was coming. Noble could see the distant line approaching. They probably would have to stop for the night and make the store tomorrow.

He set the bay into a lope. It wouldn't hurt to meet the leaders and extend an invitation to shop at the fort. Someday, he would go west—beyond the Rockies' great wall which he had never seen.

A familiar figure rode in the lead on horse back. Sudan Wilson and Rivers were returning. His spirits soaring, Noble booted the gelding into a faster run.

"Hello!" Noble shouted, reining in his horse.

"Mister Noble, you sure do look good," Sudan said with a white-toothed grin.

"Same here. I see you and Rivers are okay." He inspected the two men critically.

"We're doing fine now." Sudan laughed aloud. "But we have been worse. Say, this man with the wagon is Mr. Kitchen; he's the boss." Sudan introduced the lean, tall gray-whiskered man on the wagon seat.

"Glad to meetcha, Mr. McCurtain," Kitchen said, extending a hand. "I've heard a lot about you."

Noble shook his hand firmly. "Folks think you are pretty brave to put an outpost this far out."

Noble grinned. "Actually, the building was already here. We just added on, built up the place and laid in some supplies. These two helped me. I'm pleased to have them back," he added, smiling at Sudan and Rivers.

Sudan apparently had something on his mind. Noble could see it written on his whiskered face. He excused himself and pulled his horse beside the black man's.

"What's wrong?" Noble asked quietly.

"Yellow Deer. Is she all right?" Sudan asked anxiously.

"Sure. Take my bay and go on ahead. That horse of yours is give out?"

Sudan nodded and hesitated a moment. "I'm sorry, but we never got to Goodman. Rivers got throwed into jail; so we had to come home."

"Jail?"

"Yeah." Sudan glanced over his shoulder to make sure no one could overhear them. "They need a new lock on that Arkansas jail." Both men laughed.

"We'll have time to talk," Noble assured him as he dismounted. "Go ahead and take my horse and go see your woman."

"Yes, sir!" A broad smile crossed the black man's face.

After a visit with Kitchen, who planned to stop for a day at the store to repair and stock up, Noble and Rivers rode towards home.

"That man up there," Noble said, pointing toward Fortney, who was driving his team and stock afoot, "he hates Indians."

"Like hating Goodman," Rivers said.

"I'm not sure it's the same," Noble said slowly. "He's a strange man."

"I need a new rifle. The man in Arkansas took mine."

"We'll get you one," Noble said, reading the hidden meaning in River's words.

"In two days, I will go to Fort Smith," the Osage declared.

"Wait, Rivers. You don't understand white man's law. In Arkansas you can't kill an enemy."

The Osage nodded. "I know. I will go find him, then you can come."

"Promise me?"

"Yes, I know what they do to Indians that get mad."

"We'll get you supplies and a good horse."

"This time I will go like an eagle, slow and search out my prey."

"Yes, like an eagle," Noble echoed drily. He let Rivers ride ahead of him through the gates, pleased that all of the Osages were coming to greet their returning tribesman. With a smile of approval, Noble left the Indians and rode on to the stables.

"Noble!" Luke came shouting. "Sudan's back."

"Yes, I know, Luke." He unsaddled Sudan's thin, spent horse. "Did you speak to him?"

"Just a bit." Luke came closer and wrinkled his nose thoughtfully. "He was too busy squeezing Yellow Deer to pay attention to me."

Noble stifled a laugh. "That's the way men are with women, son."

"Yeah, I reckon so. But at least he's home again."

"Sure. Let's go up to the house." Noble was amused to see the back pounding and laughter was still going on with Rivers and the Osages. The man was obviously depressed by his failure to catch up with Goodman. Perhaps his people would cheer him up.

"Were there any boys my age with the wagon train that Sudan said was coming?"

Luke's question drew Noble's thoughts away from Rivers. "I think so."

"Good. Now that the Wichitas are gone, my friend Red Elk isn't here. It'll be nice to make new friends."

Noble looked at the boy with sympathy. It must be lonely for Luke at times.

"Noble?" Luke stopped him just before they entered the house. "You know those girls with that man Lincoln-whatever, they seem...strange. What's wrong with them?''

"What do you mean?" Noble asked sharply, surprised by the boy's perception.

"They aren't friendly. I rode down there to be neighborly; I thought maybe his boy would be there.''

"And?''

"Noble, they don't act like other settlers.'' He scowled and scuffed the toe of his boot on the porch. "I don't know exactly.''

Noble sighed. "Well, Luke, I'm afraid I don't understand them either. Don't worry about it. Come on. Let's wash up.'' Noble followed the boy inside, deciding that he would have to speak to Fleta about the Indian-hater's girls.

Later that night in their bed, Noble repeated the story about the Lincolnshire party to Fleta.

"Lots of girls in the hills marry very young, often to older men,'' she said reasonably. "Older men usually are more settled, have property, and a way to support a wife.''

"I just wondered why he thinks Indians are diseased?''

Fleta expelled a deep breath and snuggled against him. "I think he hates everybody and everything. He's not a pleasant man.''

"You may be right,'' he said absently. "We'll fix his wagon and then he can be on his way.''

"Good riddance,'' she said as she moved into his arms.

The following morning, Noble had Sudan begin work on Fortney's wheel. Noble felt an urgency to get the man off his property.

Luke came by to saddle his pinto. He spoke briefly to both men then rode out to meet the approaching wagon train. Spotted Horse and Barge came to join them in the rough board smithy shed.

"Rivers talked to you about leaving, Noble?'' Spotted Horse asked.

"Yes,'' Noble looked at him sharply. "Has he left already?''

"No, he is still sleeping.''

"Good. I want to remind him he's not to harm Goodman, only find him and let me know. I'll handle Izer when Rivers finds the bastard.''

Spotted Horse nodded. "I will be sure he understands.''

"He can have whatever supplies he needs.''

The chief grunted. "If not for Sudan, he would be in the iron door box. He learned he will have to have your help."

"Good." Noble was satisfied Rivers knew his ways would not work outside the fort.

Evening came with a slowly sinking sun. In the interval, the wagon train people had frequented the store, purchasing supplies by the crateful. Mr. Kitchen accepted an invitation to eat dinner with the McCurtains. The two men were drinking tea while Fleta cleared the table.

"How bad are the Indians west of here?" Kitchen asked.

"There's been a lot of talk about trouble brewing. Bands will be coming south to meet the main herd of buffalo, because folks have killed so many. There use to be a lot more here. Right, Fleta?"

She smiled. "We ate a lot of it the first two years we were here."

"I see," Kitchen said. "I'll keep an eye out. There's lots of talk. I don't want my people upset but still I need them ready in case."

Noble agreed. Rumors were all he heard. All the Indians so far had been peaceful enough, but there was no assurance that they would remain so. A little whiskey had turned the placid Wichitas into crazy ones. Even the Army with its more frequent patrols now seemed convinced that spring would bring increased problems in the far western parts of Kansas.

"Noble, come quick!" Luke shouted from outside. He rushed to the open doorway. "That crazy man Lincoln-whatever is beating his wives with a whip."

"Wives?" Noble stood up, his expression puzzled.

"Yeah." Luke said, panting for breath. "I found out both of them girls are his wives."

"What the hell kind of man is he?" Kitchen asked, frowning at Noble while they stood facing each other undecidedly.

"Damned if I know." Noble shrugged, wondering what would happen next.

"Wait," Fleta said as they moved toward the door. "I'm coming with you." She grabbed her shawl from the hook by the door and wrapped it around her shoulders.

Kitchen, Noble, and Fleta confronted Fortney, with Luke a respectable distance behind. Smothered sounds of the girl's sobs came from within the wagon behind him.

"Just what is going on here?" Noble demanded, squinting at the man's silhouette outlined by the campfire.

"This is my business, Mr. McCurtain," Fortney said flatly.

"Do you have two wives?" Noble asked.

"Are you the law?" The man challenged defensively.

"By God, we're asking the questions here," Kitchen said.

Fortney drew back his shoulders. "There's no law against it."

"We want to speak to them." Fleta spoke for the first time. The whimpering from the wagon pulled at her heartstrings. She glared at the man icily, hoping it would shrivel him despite the fire behind his back.

"It's none of your business, Madam. I have papers to show that I married both of them legally. When my wife died, I married them. They were her girls by her first marriage."

Fleta blinked in shock, incapable of saying anything. She looked at Noble helplessly.

"Mr. Lincolnshire, I'm going to have your wagon wheel fixed in the morning. Until then, this is my land and I won't tolerate you beating up any women here. Do you understand?"

"You ain't—"

"On this land, I am the law, Mister," Noble cut him off. "And I will personally horsewhip you if you lay another hand on those girls." Noble towered over the smaller man, waiting for a reply. When Fortney did not speak, but sucked in his cheeks gustily, Noble added, "Mister, do you understand what I'm saying?"

"Yeah, yeah, I hear you," Lincolnshire said sullenly.

"Then remember it well," Noble warned. He put his arm around Fleta's shoulders and escorted her with the others back toward the store.

"Damned polygamist," Kitchen muttered in disgust.

"Worse than that," Fleta said. "A wife beater. How old is the youngest girl?"

"Fleta, there ain't one damn thing I can do except to keep him from beating them while they're here."

"I know, I know." She jerked away and wrapped the shawl tighter, a sick feeling settling inside at her helplessness to do anything for the girls.

"Noble, why was he beating those girls?" Luke asked timidly.

"He's just plain crazy," Kitchen said flatly. "Excuse me, I'm going back to my wagon train. I sure appreciate the meal, ma'am. And it was nice to meet all of you."

"Have a safe trip. Guess you'll be leaving in the morning?" Noble asked.

"Yep, first light."

They walked in silence, Luke moving ahead.

"I just wish we could do something about him," Fleta said sadly.

Noble reached out to hug her shoulder. "So do I, sweetheart, but there really isn't anything."

Fleta nodded and leaned against him. Thank God, she had such a strong man. But even he could not resolve everything.

At daybreak, Noble sent Sudan to help Fortney get his wagon wheel. Two days passed before the wagon was repaired and Fortney was ready to move on.

Noble wanted to avoid the surly man, so he helped Rivers pack a horse with supplies.

"This pistol I traded for is as good as the ones I have, except the trigger's broken," Noble explained. "When you cock it, be ready 'cause it fires."

Rivers nodded. His brown eyes studied the revolver. Noble handed him a wooden bullet box that had a sliding top. Rivers put the Spencer repeater in the scabbard and packed away the five tubes of ammunition inside his saddle bags.

"Now, Rivers," Noble warned, "remember you just find Izer, then come back. Right?"

"Rivers send word or come quick."

Noble clapped him on the shoulder. "You're a good man."

"I will find him," Rivers said in such a solemn voice that Noble was sure the Osage would find that rotten devil.

Rivers left, cheered on by his wives, the other Osage and the yap of a few pups.

Fleta put her hand on Noble's tense back. She moved silently toward him and spoke softly, ''You're very worried, aren't you?''

He nodded, watching the rider and pack horse disappearing in the distance.

''What will happen when Rivers finds Goodman?'' she asked.

''I'll go kill him,'' Noble said flatly.

''Don't do it for me. I'm fine now,'' she said truthfully. She was no longer haunted by nightmares. She had regained her strength and could go on with her life.

''I'll do it for all of us,'' Noble vowed grimly. ''For the Osages, you and ... myself. I have to.''

Chapter Sixteen

Spring of 1868 merged into summer. Fleta studied her husband's back as he stood in the doorway. His shoulders had broadened in the time since she had first met him. The slight gray streak over his right ear was a reminder of the wound the bushwhackers had inflicted on him a few years ago.

As she fixed his breakfast, she frowned worriedly. "Noble, how serious is this Indian matter?"

Noble drew a deep breath and sipped his coffee before answering. "Most of it's in far western Kansas. Cheyenne and Sioux mostly. That's why the army is making everyone turn north to get to the Sante Fe Trail. They claim they can protect them better on that route."

"What about that Captain Rourke who was here early this morning? What did he tell you?"

Noble could not meet her probing gaze. "We just talked." He didn't want to tell her what he had learned from his friend. Earlier that week, an army patrol found a burned wagon several days west of the fort. The corpses were horribly mutilated. The descriptions matched Fortney Lincolnshire and his family. If possible, he wanted to keep the information from Fleta.

"Well, Noble? What's wrong?" she asked impatiently.

"Nothing. He just wanted to warn us to keep a close watch for trouble. Spotted Horse is riding further out that way to keep an eye out."

Fleta turned the bacon over, convinced that Noble was keeping something from her. She knew from past experience that it would do no good to try and pry it out of him. "It sounds serious. Noble, you'll have to speak to Luke. He rides that pony farther and farther every day."

"I'll talk to him," Noble promised. "By the way, Colonel Custer, the man who gave me the gray stallion, is coming here in a couple of weeks."

"Oh?"

"Rourke says that the colonel wants me to accompany them for a ways."

"A ways? Just how far is that?"

Noble picked up his coffee cup and started across the room with it. He stopped at the window and stared out across the compound. "I'm not sure. I didn't say I would go."

"But," Fleta inserted with a hint of irritation, "I expect you'll go all the same,"

Noble turned to look at her. "Do you mind?"

"No, not really," she said, her voice filled with resignation. "Just don't expect me to be happy about you leaving."

"I doubt you'll have any problems while I'm gone. Besides, we need to stay on the good side of the military. If settlers are turned back east of here, we could lose a lot of business."

Fleta pierced the bacon angrily, causing a dot of hot grease to splash on her finger. She cursed under her breath. Although the burn was minor, she felt close to tears.

Noble watched her for a moment, torn with indecision. He wanted to pull her into his arms and tell her that he would not go, but he had a responsibility to the military and to the store's best interest. Scowling, he put his cup down on the table and spoke without looking at her. "I'll go speak to Luke now."

"Fine. Breakfast is about ready. Bring him back with you so he can eat," she said stiffly. When he left the room. Fleta's shoulders slumped. He intended to go with Custer and there wasn't a thing she could do to persuade him otherwise. Besides, it seemed that something else was bothering Noble. It couldn't be the store, she mused. The profits had been unbelievable for the past year. They had more money saved than she would have dreamed possible. Maybe Noble was worried about Rivers?

Two weeks later, Custer's Seventh Cavalry approached the fort. Noble watched the long line of cavalry from a small hill. Flags and guidons waved; the dust of the supply ambulances rose behind the double columns.

The Seventh was impressive from his vantage point. Certainly a much greater force than the small patrols that diverted the wagon trains north. Noble understood why the proclamation was so hated by the settlers, the detour meant a week or two longer journey.

When Noble rode down to join the cavalry, he immediately noticed the prominent figure in front, wearing buckskins. He checked the gray and stopped to watch the procession. Custer had a reputation for being eccentric. A pair of whippets, used to hunt coyotes and rabbits, padded alongside Custer's horse.

Noble wondered about the man. Custer had been a general once, although his peacetime rank was lower. Would the colonel ask about his own military service or non-service? Rumors had it the man planned to run for President. A small flutter of anxiety began in Noble's stomach. How would he measure up to such an impressive figure as Custer?

Captain Rourke rode out to greet him. "Good day, Noble. The colonel is honored that you're coming to meet him."

Noble nodded. "Thanks. I was out checking my stock when I caught sight of you all coming." He fell in beside Rourke and rode back to meet Custer.

The colonel was easily recognizable by his long golden hair and matching mustache. He removed a fringed buckskin gauntlet and extended a hand to Noble.

"McCurtain, at last we meet," the man said with a very slight smile. "I see you've taken excellent care of Salizar," he said.

"I'm grateful for the horse. Some day I'll have a colt good enough to repay you."

"Fine idea. Ride along with us and we'll visit," Custer invited. "We intend to camp outside your place tonight."

"You're more than welcome," Noble said, glad he had already warned Spotted Horse about the cavalry. He didn't anticipate any problems from the Indians.

Noble fell into line beside the colonel and watched the soldiers ahead. The scouts rode in a group apart from the troopers. Most of the scouts were dressed in soiled leather, almost tattered compared to Custer's immaculate outfit. The men reminded him of Izer Goodman in their style of dress. Although he scrutinized the scouts keenly, he did not recognize any of them. He wondered, for what seemed like the hundredth time, where Izer Goodman was. Why hadn't Rivers brought back word about the damned outlaw?

"I have some plans to discuss with you," Custer said, breaking in on his thoughts. "I hope you'll consider joining me on this campaign," Custer continued in an almost paternal tone.

Noble had been expecting the question. His hands tightened on the reins and he peered sideways at the man. "How long will it require? I hate to be gone a long time from my business and livestock."

Custer's blue eyes seemed intent on something on the horizon. Apparently he was deep in thought. Eventually he spoke in a slow, measured tone. "My scouts tell me there is a large band of troublemakers camped a few hard days march west of your place at Cottonwood Forks. Perhaps, two hundred or more bucks. They're killing and drying buffalo for winter food. If we capture their food supply and defeat them, they'd quit this winter and come in or starve."

"What tribes?" Noble asked warily.

"Sioux, Cheyenne, even some Pawnee." Custer looked at Rourke for more information.

"Iron Kettle is one of the chiefs," Rourke supplied.

"Yes," Custer said with a frown. "I would like that old fox in irons."

"Why do you need me?" Noble asked bluntly.

Custer's brows rose and he turned to look at Noble with an aloof expression. Then his face cleared and he spoke with what seemed like forced persuasion, "Congress has become penny tight toward our campaign to resettle these renegades. A successful foray against these hostiles and a favorable report from a prominent citizen might impress some of those lily-livered officials who think the whole Indian matter will simply go away if they ignore it." The man's nostrils flared with contempt as he finished his speech.

Noble now understood his position. He was to be a verifier of the Seventh's action so the military could requisition more funds.

The colonel was convinced the Indians were only going to stop attacking if they realized they faced a stronger opposing force. Noble dismissed his own doubts. Custer was a military leader; he was only a store keeper and stock raiser. Who was he to question such an expert?

"I understand from Captain Rourke that you have a lovely wife, Mr. McCurtain." Custer said.

"Yes," Noble said shortly, wondering why the man was interested in his marital status.

"Then you must bring her to my tent for supper. My own wife Libby is back east visiting relatives, so the company of an attractive lady at supper will be a welcome diversion from the world of men."

A jealous chord plucked at Noble. Custer might rule an army, but he needn't think he would have any special privileges where Fleta was concerned.

"The meal will be at seven," Custer said.

"All right." Noble wasn't sure that he wanted Fleta anywhere near the fancy commander. "I'll have to ask my wife," he added.

"Certainly. I can promise you she will enjoy the musicians. And my cook is famous. Even under such primitive conditions as we have out here, he can create a culinary masterpiece."

"I'm sure my wife will be flattered," Noble said stiffly. "I'll ride ahead and warn her of the plans. You know how women can be about surprises."

"Of course. Send the fair lady my compliments, and I'll look for both of you around seven."

"Yes." Noble started to turn the gray away.

"McCurtain?" Custer stopped him. "You are seriously considering joining the Seventh on this campaign, aren't you?"

Noble pursed his lips. He owed the man for the great horse. A week of his own time would be payment enough for the stallion. "Yes, I'm considering it."

"Good." Custer smiled, a small polite courtesy he could now afford once he had gotten his way.

Back at the store, Noble followed Fleta toward the new addition to the house. "I'm not sure I want you to attend this fancy dinner."

"You said you wanted both of us to go." She turned and looked at him in puzzlement. "What's wrong?"

Noble shrugged. "I don't trust the man," he said flatly.

"You what?" Fleta had a hard time hiding a smile at Noble's aggressive tone.

"You heard me. He's a powerful man."

"Noble, what are you talking about?"

"I think the son-of-a-bitch could sweep any woman he wanted off her feet."

Fleta laughed softly, amused by the petulant expression on his face. "Why, Noble McCurtain, are you jealous?"

He shifted his weight from his toes to his heels. "I don't want him stealing you."

Fleta was deeply moved by his confession. "Oh, Noble, no one is going to steal me." She took his arm and pulled him toward the kitchen. "Just let the colonel try. He won't impress me that much."

"Fleta, I'd..."

"Noble," she looked up at him sternly. "Promise me you won't behave aggressively."

"All right, all right. But that doesn't mean I have to like it."

"Remember," she warned him. "Custer can turn the settlers north where ever he wants to. We have to keep on his good side. We just have to show a little diplomacy and tact."

Noble's brows raised and he smiled at his wife. "I'll try," he promised.

But a little later, when Fleta turned before him in her new tan dress, he wasn't so sure he was going to be able to keep his word. She was as pretty as any fancy woman he had ever seen. Her auburn hair was curled into shiny ringlets and her dress molded her supple breasts and slender hips. He ran his finger around his stiff celluloid collar and scowled. How was any man supposed to keep his hands off Fleta when she looked so enticing?

When Fleta finally met Colonel Custer, she was impressed with his worldly manner and stylish dress. He greeted her with great charm, kissing the back of her hand while Noble glowered at him. During the excellent meal of prairie chicken in wine sauce, Custer rose twice to toast her beauty. The crystal glasses clinked together musically. Fleta kept her eyes lowered to the long, lavishly spread table. The starched white linen and delicate china plates brought a thrill of delight to her. More so than did the womanizing Custer. She sipped the red wine, sending Noble a smile of assurance. The smile stayed on her lips as she wondered how Custer's staff managed to crate around the fragile dishes without breaking them.

The soft notes from the musicians' violins were almost hypnotizing. She closed her eyes and grasped Noble's hand under the table, giving it a gentle squeeze. Immediately she felt him relax.

"Mrs. McCurtain, do you enjoy prairie life?" Custer asked as the meal continued.

Fleta looked at him frankly. "Oh yes, I do. We have a good business here."

"Oh, yes?" Custer sounded slightly disapproving. "You manage the store, I understand."

"Yes." Fleta added a smile to soften the brief answer.

Custer clicked his tongue and leaned back in his chair, studying the contents of his wine glass. "Women on the frontier seem to take on many new roles. Roles of independence, I would say."

"Perhaps," Fleta murmured. "Is that such a bad thing, Colonel?" she dared to ask.

Custer laughed a low rumble, "Touche. Do I detect a drawl in your voice, Madam?"

With difficulty, she kept the smile on her face and gave Noble another reassuring squeeze from her hand. What was Custer getting at? she wondered. "Yes, I'm from northern Arkansas. I met Noble there."

"You have a son, I believe?"

Fighting the urge to tell the arrogant man it was none of his business, Fleta dabbed the linen napkin at her mouth and gave him a direct look. "Yes, by a previous marriage,"

"Ah, you're a war widow?" he probed.

"Yes." Out of the corner of her eye, Fleta noted Noble's impatient movement.

"I'm sorry about you loss, Madam. Which side was he on?" Custer asked.

"The South," Fleta answered, cursing the shaky note in her voice. What was the man trying to prove? He was deliberately intimidating with his softly spoken probes.

"Yes, there were far too many men lost on both sides. McCurtain, you seem to have lost your drawl."

Fleta forced a laugh. "Unless he's contracted mine, he wouldn't have one. Noble's from Illinois."

"Ah." Custer lifted his hands and smiled benignly. "Strange things happen during war times. It seems to bring people from afar together. Fortunately for you, Mr. McCurtain," he added with a charming smile.

"Yes." Noble said briefly, his eyes narrowed in growing aggression.

"Colonel, you must raise a lot of good horses like the gray that you so generously gave to my husband," Fleta said, hoping to redirect the conversation.

Custer did not immediately rise to the bait. "Yes," he said slowly, taking his eyes from Noble's face. "I keep an eye out for good ones. Being in the military, I naturally have a talent for choosing the right kind of remounts," he said with a trace of smugness.

"How interesting." Fleta batted her lashes at him, hoping to keep his thoughts off her personal life and Noble's military service. "I suppose someday you'll raise them on your own?"

"Oh, perhaps some day I will. I love the military, serving my fellow man, and developing the country out here. I offer my leadership to the cause."

"Oh," Fleta breathed with a forced sigh of admiration. Inside she was wrinkling her nose with distaste at the pompous statement. But if he wanted to brag about himself, that was better than probing at Noble's service record or the lack of one.

"Would you dance with me, Mrs. McCurtain?" Custer asked and rose. "I see you are not eating."

"I-I'm not sure." She looked at Noble for guidance.

"McCurtain, may I dance with your lovely wife?" Custer asked with the tone of a man who is unaccustomed to be denied.

"If she wishes to." Noble swirled the wine in his glass, refusing to meet Fleta's imploring gaze.

Fleta was upset with his reply. Then she realized Noble was simply doing as she had requested. If he had told the colonel no, what might that have led to? It was only one dance, after all. Before she could ask Noble if he really minded, Rourke, on Noble's right began a serious conversation with him.

Fleta put down her napkin and rose uncertainly as Custer offered to take her chair. "I doubt that I will be anything but clumsy, Colonel. It has been a long time since I've danced."

"Oh, I sincerely doubt you could ever by anything but graceful, Mrs. McCurtain." He held out his hand and led her to a small wooden platform on the other side of the tent.

The man thought of everything, she mused with grudging admiration. His hand on her waist was firm and strong as he led her to the dance floor.

She was propelled around in a box waltz that she vaguely recalled dancing years before. Custer was so completely in command she began to doubt her power to hold him at bay. Her feet followed his smoothly; she felt a smile tug at her mouth, and wondered if half a glass of wine had intoxicated her more than she realized. George Armstrong Custer was all that Noble had suspected and more.

From the corner of her eye, Fleta noted Custer's staff had Noble fully occupied. Custer's plan was so obvious she felt a twinge of amusement.

"Shall we step outside? It'll be cooler out of this tent," Custer murmured softly.

"All right," Fleta agreed, with a seed of curiosity as to what Custer might try next.

A cool breeze floated across the prairie, disturbing the wispy tendrils of Fleta's hair. She lifted her face and stared up at the stars.

"Your husband seemed reluctant to allow you out of his sight," Custer said with a superior smile in his voice.

A sigh of resentment escaped Fleta. She was beginning to grow weary of Custer's pompous attitude. "Colonel, I think my husband feels he owes you for the horse."

In the light from the tent, she could see a scowl of irritation flash across the man's face. "Forget about the horse. I need McCurtain to convince Congress how important my work here is."

"I see." And Fleta was beginning to see just what the man was angling after. He obviously wanted her to persuade Noble to put in a good report about the Seventh Cavalry. She looked at the colonel wordlessly, wondering just how far he would exercise his great charm in order to get her on his side.

"The military needs more funds," he continued, "in order to bring peace to the region. We must have sufficient backing in order to do our job properly." He cupped her elbow with his hand and steered her away from the tent.

"Aren't the stars magnificent out here?" he asked, drawing in a deep breath.

"Kansas certainly has its share," she agreed.

Custer dropped his hand from her elbow and stood looking down at her averted face. "You seem very confident, Mrs. McCurtain. May I call you Fleta?"

She looked at her hands in the starlight. "I don't think that would be very wise, Colonel."

"Pity. You are obviously accustomed to dealing with men," he said.

"I suppose that comes from working in the store. In the past few years, I've become comfortable talking to men. As long as they respect me," she added pointedly.

"But of course. We could not help but respect and greatly admire such beauty as yours," he said smoothly. "I must say that I didn't expect such charm and strength from a woman living in such an isolated area."

Fleta laughed softly. "You thought such a woman would swoon at your feet because of your beautiful manners, your delicious dinner, and romantic music?"

Custer laughed aloud. "You remind me very much of my Libby."

"Thank you."

"I can see that you have my measure, dear lady. Perhaps we feel a kinship?"

Fleta looked at him blankly. When he put both of his hands on her arms and gently tugged her closer, she stared at him aghast.

"May I kiss you?"

She looked up at him levelly. "No, I don't think that would be wise either, Colonel. You did say you wanted my husband's support?"

His hands fell away and his head reared back slightly as if in deep surprise.

"Colonel, I think we should return to the tent. No doubt, by now my husband has heard all of Captain Rourke's stories."

"Very well, Mrs. McCurtain," he said stiffly.

Fleta picked up her skirt slightly and turned back toward the camp. "Oh, I think you can make it Fleta now, Colonel."

A small laugh of grudging admiration left Custer's mouth. "Fleta. Charming name for a shrewd, charming woman."

"Touche," Fleta said with a soft laugh as they reached the tent opening.

Fleta and Noble were silent on the way home. When they reached the store, Noble was uncertain whether to ask her what had transpired between her and the great commander. As she undressed, he watched her through narrow eyes, jealousy gnawing at his insides.

"Just what went on when Custer waltzed you outside?"

Fleta stifled a sigh. She knew Noble would question her about their absence, but truthfully, she was tired and just a little sick of hearing about the great Colonel Custer. "Nothing happened, Noble," she said wearily.

"You must have enjoyed it."

"Oh, must I?" she retorted.

"Don't be coy."

She sat on the bed, letting her hairbrush fall to the floor. "I am not being coy. I was wined, dined, and danced by a man whom I suspect could someday be the President of the United States."

"Oh?" Noble tucked his thumbs in his belt loop and stared down at the top of her shiny head.

"Yes and that was all. Noble McCurtain, nothing happened." She glared up at him, wondering if they were going to have their very first fight over some arrogant womanizer. "Colonel Custer is far too vain a person to interest me. Now are you coming to bed with me or do you wish to stay up all night, worrying about something that never happened?"

A slow grin spread over his mouth. He leaned forward and kissed her firmly. "I'm still glad that he's leaving at dawn."

"Oh! Are you going with him?"

"Yes, I gave my word, Fleta."

She closed her eyes, knowing that nothing she could say would dissuade him. To Noble, his word was everything. "Well, let's not spend your last night arguing. Come to bed," she said softly.

"Yes, ma'am."

The Seventh Cavalry moved out at dawn. Noble was not long in their company when he began to see that Custer was a stern taskmaster. Judging by the way he pushed his men and their mounts, the great leader would stop at nothing in order to accomplish his mission. Noble listened to the reports that the scouts brought back concerning the Indians camp at Cottonwood Forks. The army continued to push westward, stopping only for a brief cold meal.

Rourke explained the reason for the cold meals. "Fire smoke is a dead giveaway. Our dust is bad enough. We can only hope they think we're buffalo herds moving."

Seasoned, tough veterans, who muttered only an occasional complaint, made up the Seventh. Hard voiced non-coms shouted commands. Noble decided he had missed little in not having military experience.

Noble watched a trooper carry his government saddle, bedroll, and gear toward an ambulance. Defeat etched the man's face, for he no longer could ride with his fellow troopers. He was doomed to ride a wagon. Horse care seemed the worry of every man. They lost several animals in the forced march.

Grateful for the powerful gray, Noble saw no signs of him tiring.

"Well?" Custer asked, riding up beside him, "What do you think of the Seventh now?"

"They are certainly well-trained veterans."

"Yes, they are. With enough appropriations, we can end all hostilities from here to Canada in two years."

"I imagine you could."

"My scouts tell me if we continue to ride all night, by dawn we can be within striking distance of our enemies."

Noble nodded, not trusting himself to speak. He knew what the colonel meant. If they rode a bunch more horses in the ground, they'd be there at sunrise. It was a damned shame to ride good horses to death, but he knew the colonel wouldn't appreciate him saying so.

"Do you approve?"

"I don't know anything about Indian warfare," Noble said tactfully.

"You are quite honest, McCurtain, for a civilian."

"Thanks," Noble said dryly. "Don't worry about the gray and me. We'll make it there."

The colonel turned to study the line of troops coming behind them. "Were you ever a soldier?"

Well, the question was out. Noble was tired of side stepping the issue. He looked at the man frankly. "No."

Custer turned and gazed at him with an almost pitying smile. "Well, come dawn you'll see the Seventh in action." He slapped his leg in anticipation. "By damn, I think you'll be impressed."

"I'm sure I will, Colonel." Noble was glad when the commander left. The man now knew that he had never fought in the war; he probably suspected it all along. But what difference did it make? All Custer needed, Noble reminded himself sourly, was a good report from a prominent citizen. He rubbed his stubbled jaw, wondering why Custer did not have a newsman along on the trip. A man like him should have as many as two or three reporters, taking notes of his heroic actions. Why, Rourke sometimes even brought reporters with him on a patrol. Custer was up to something, and somehow Noble felt that he was part of the plot.

The push through the night wearied Noble and the stallion. Short breaks and tepid chalky water did little to revive them. His eyes burned from lack of sleep. Even the stallion seemed listless as he plodded along.

A fresh night wind bathed Noble's face as Rourke drew to his side.

"You are to wait here," Rourke said. "The colonel has given orders to hold our fire unless shot at. He is giving the enemy a chance to surrender."

Noble nodded. He listened to muffled sounds of troopers, punctuated with an occasional horse snort. He didn't have the slightest doubt that a precision military lineup was taking place in the darkness.

Dawn was about to shatter the night. Rourke had ridden off to join his outfit. Noble could see the long double line of cavalry stretched out. Below them, he could see the forks of two streams and the outline of some spindly cottonwoods. The peaks of several tepees seemed far away, yet Noble knew they weren't more than one-third of a mile from the troopers.

He heard the distant yap of Indian dogs, shattered by the bugler's blast. In front, there was a sword-wielding officer, then the entire wave moved forward at a gallop. Considering their horses' tired condition, Noble was amazed. Custer's reserves stood still as the first troop swept down the slope. The bugle's 'Charge' sounded across the land.

A thunder of hundreds of horses shook the earth as they bore down on the Indian camp. What was it Rourke said—that hostile Indians were to be given the chance to surrender—that must be Custer's little joke.

A round of scattered shots filled the morning air. They were answered by a volley of the trooper's fire. The Indians had chosen to fight.

Who wouldn't have fought? Noble wondered with cynicism. Hundreds of troopers with ear-shattering bugles bearing down on a sleeping village was enough to make anyone stand up and fight.

Screams, shouts, and gunshots carried across the land. Noble did not watch the battle. He led the gray toward the wagon with the water barrel. After getting a drink, he fed and watered his horse, then led him away from the soldiers and searched for a place to sleep. Somewhere away from all the death.

He jerked at the rolling voice commanding the reserves to join the battle. Custer's backup was going in to assist. Noble's teeth ground together as he heard the screams from below. He walked back over to the water wagon to get more of the taste out of his mouth.

"Hell," he swore aloud.

"That's right, sir. To have to stay up here and miss a damned good fight is hell."

Noble looked at the lean-jawed soldier who came up behind him. He surmised the young soldier had lost his horse on the way and that was why he was being left behind with the wagon.

"I guess it would be hell for a soldier," Noble agreed, turning on a wooden spigot to fill a canvas bucket. The Seventh could use the Indians' blood to quench their thirst riding back. Enough was being spilled down there to water a desert.

"Custer is a tough man, but he's always damned sure where the action is," the trooper said.

"What else do you do when you aren't fighting Injuns?"

"Stable duty. Train for battle. Hell, I hate missing one like this."

Compared to the other two duties, Noble understood how Indian warfare might be a relief.

The shots and screams lessened. He was glad. He didn't want to think about the dead women and children. When a final count of the dead was made, the innocent bystanders would likely be lumped together with the others. Custer wouldn't care how many women and children were killed while the Seventh was dealing with the so-called hostile elements. Noble sighed tiredly. He would write the report that Custer wanted, but he would not add his own editorial comments to it. He had a sick feeling that it wouldn't make much difference even if he did.

"Well sounds like we did it." The soldier beamed.

"Yeah, we did it, didn't we?" Noble said, his voice full of irony. "Tell Captain Rourke I'll be out there sleeping somewhere if he needs me."

"Sure, but ain't you riding down and getting some Injun things? There'll be women," the man added with a leering grin.

"No," Noble said through clenched teeth. "I think I'll pass on that."

Chapter Seventeen

Sudan stood beside Fleta, watching the Seventh Cavalry leave. "Misses, Noble will be back before you know it."

"I hope so, Sudan," Fleta said, turning away. Her legs were leaden as she walked back to the store.

Sudan went back to his blacksmithing, there was plenty of work to do. He had to make some hinges and repair a wagon brake rod. As he fired the forge, he wondered about Noble. How would Noble get along with that yellow-haired Colonel? There was a strained atmosphere between them, though Sudan did not know why.

Yellow Deer brought him a canvas pail of fresh water. He wiped his perspiring forehead with the back of his hand.

Out of the corner of his eye, he caught sight of an approaching rider. Moving out of the shed that housed his forge, he watched the man ride through the gate. The stranger was an Indian, dressed in white man's clothes.

"Who's that?" He asked Yellow Deer, making sure his rifle was nearby. The women shook her head. Sudan stripped off his leather apron, then walked toward the stranger.

"Are you Noble McCurtain?" The man asked Sudan as he dismounted.

"No." Sudan was glad when Spotted Horse joined him. "I work for Mr. McCurtain."

"Where is he?" The man looked around expectantly.

Fleta came out on the porch. "What's wrong?"

Sudan glanced at her as he answered. "This man wants Noble."
He turned back to the stranger. "He won't be back for a while.
Can we help you?"

"An Osage by the name of Rivers send me here with a message
for Noble McCurtain. He said McCurtain would pay me."

Sudan frowned. "Is Rivers all right?" he demanded sharply.

The man shrugged. "He's fine. He said you would pay me
forty dollars to ride here."

"Sudan, what's he saying?" Fleta shouted.

Sudan turned to her. "He has a message from Rivers, but we
need to pay him."

Fleta waved her hand. "We'll pay him."

"You heard her. What's the message?" Sudan asked.

"Izer Coldman is at Fort Smith."

Fleta heard the words. Despite the man's mispronunciation, she
felt sure he meant Izer Goodman. Filled with apprehension, she
was certain when Noble heard the news, he would immediately
leave for Fort Smith. She glared at the Indian, wishing he had never
appeared.

Realizing that the three men were looking at her expectantly,
she shook her head and mumbled she would get the man's money.
As she fumbled in the cashbox, she railed against the unkind fate
that had dealt her such an unfair hand. Bad enough Noble was off
fighting with Custer. Now Izer Goodman had turned up again.
Would their life never be settled?

Sudan learned that the messenger's name was Charlie Horseman.
He invited the visitor to come to his tepee for some food.

Charlie looked around, then put a hand on Sudan's arm before
entering the tent. "Are all the buffalo gone?" he asked in a hushed
whisper.

The black man laughed. "No."

"Good." The Cherokee nodded his satisfaction, then followed
Sudan inside the tepee.

The following week passed slowly for Fleta. She stood firm about
Charlie leaving. After pressing two twenty-dollar gold pieces into
Sudan's hand to give to the man, she demanded he send Charlie
on his way before Noble returned.

In the middle of the week, Fleta confronted her son about his habit of riding his pony all over the countryside. "You cannot ride all over Kansas by yourself as you have been doing, Luke. There could be savages anywhere. Why do you think Noble is out with the army?"

"Aw, ma! I ain't scared."

"That's not the point, Luke," she said sharply. How he could have grown up so fast without her noticing? "You are to stay in the fort. No more riding Shaw all over until Noble returns."

"Oh no!"

"Yes." She drew in a deep breath and straightened her shoulders, determined to be firm with her impetuous son. "When Noble returns, we'll see what he has to say about the matter. Until then do as I say. Do you understand?"

"Yes." Luke's shoulders slumped in defeat. With a scowl of irritation, he tugged on Shaw's reins to lead him back to the corral.

Later in the day, Spotted Horse brought news of an approaching wagon train. Mannah helped Fleta straighten the store in readiness for the customers. Sudan moved some heavy items for them so they could restock the depleted shelves.

"Rivers won't do anything foolish while he waits, will he?" she asked Sudan.

"No. Charlie Horseman will explain to him that Noble is coming. Rivers knows about the problems he could have if he tries to take Izer alone."

Fleta was filled with dread—Noble would ride on to Fort Smith, the moment he returned from Custer's campaign.

"You are worrying again," Mannah scolded her. "There is no need."

Fleta blinked in surprise. "I'm just upset about Noble being gone."

"I know." The woman put an arm on her shoulder briefly.

Fleta smiled. "Very well, Mannah. I won't borrow any more trouble. Thank you."

The people from the wagon train came to shop in hordes during the late evening. One women dithered about some calico material. Fleta waited patiently for her to make up her mind. A man entered the store, causing Fleta's eyes to widen and her heart to pound in her chest.

Wilbourne Corey stood in front of her.

Fleta swallowed with difficulty, hoping she wasn't as pale as she felt.

"May—may I help you?" She mumbled through trembling lips.

"Needle and thread," he said, his small eyes boring a hole in her face.

If she hadn't been so frightened, Fleta would have laughed at the absurd conversation she and her erstwhile husband were having. "How many needles?" she asked.

"My wife said two."

Fleta blinked at him in astonishment. Had Wilbourne remarried? A wave of nausea swept her. Her fingers fumbled in the sewing supplies. She managed to withdraw two needles.

"What color thread?" she asked in a hoarse whisper, feeling alternately relieved and outraged at the news of his marriage.

"White's fine." He followed and stood behind her, making her feel as if she were suffocating. "The boy outside," Wilbourne asked in a low voice, "is our son?"

Fleta's eyes widened when she comprehended the fact. "Yes, that's Luke."

Wilbourne stepped back so she could pass. She put the needles and thread together in a stiff piece of brown paper and wrapped them carefully. When he reached into his pocket to pay her, she shook her head, refusing to accept his money.

Wilbourne looked around the store. Fleta studied him. His face was weathered and he looked much older than she remembered. His shoulders were rounded and his stomach bulged. And she noted, with satisfaction, that he had a decidedly weak chin.

As if he felt her eyes upon him, he jerked around and looked at her keenly. "You look just as I remembered you," he said softly.

"You too," she lied, wishing he would disappear again.

"I have a new wife," he said with a touch of smugness. "Do you remember Madeline Bower?"

Fleta shook her head and clenched her teeth to steady her trembling lips. "I—I hope you're happy, Wilbourne."

"I nearly came here once to take you back home." He searched around again, as if suspecting Noble was somewhere nearby.

"He's not here; he's gone with the army. Your train will have to turn north here. It's an order of the military."

Wilbourne nodded. "We already knew that. We're going to California."

Fleta fought the guilt and the anger. She closed her eyes, envisioning Noble's strong face. A feeling of relief assailed her when she opened her eyes and looked at the man who had been her husband. "Do you need any money?"

"No,"

"Are you sure?" she persisted.

"I don't wany any of your damned blood money," he snarled, slapping a dime on the counter for his purchases.

She flinched at the sound and stared up at him in puzzlement. "What do you mean blood money?"

Wilbourne smirked and shook his head. "I know how you started this place. Blood money from bushwhacking your own people."

"That's a lie!" she hissed, her eyes sparkling with anger.

"I know the damned truth. God will judge your wicked ways, Fleta!" Wilbourne pronounced in a self-righteous tone. He turned and strode quickly out the door.

Fleta hurried after him, wanting to thump him for slurring Noble. A moment of panic struck her as she realized that Luke was outside. She watched anxiously as Wilbourne stared at the unaware Luke, who was practicing with his lariat by the corral. Fleta hands clenched. Surely he would not try to take Luke with him?

When Wilbourne turned and walked through the gateway toward a wagon, she nearly fainted with relief.

"Who's he?" Mannah asked from behind her.

"A dead man," Fleta said flatly. She was amazed at the great wave of peacefulness that flooded her. Wilbourne was leaving, out of her life forever, she prayed.

Noble returned two days later on the jaded, gray stallion. Fleta was grateful that Wilbourne's train had left. When he dismounted, she rushed to be in his embrace.

"Is something wrong?" he asked, looking down on her head.

She buried her face in his shirt. The strong smell of horse and sweat filled her nose—she clung to him, grateful for his safe return.

He finally held her out at arms length. "Is everyone all right?"

Fleta smiled through her tears. "Yes, now you're home."

Noble smiled at Luke, who had come up to greet him.

"Where's Colonel Custer?" the boy asked.

"They headed home. I came straight here."

"Did you find the bad Indians, Noble?" he asked eagerly.

"They did." Noble tried to contain his true feelings.

"Wow, I wish I could have gone with you. Now can I ride Shaw outside the fort?"

"Sure, Luke." He frowned privately at Fleta for why the boy asked his permission.

"Ma was afraid the savages would get me," Luke said, kicking the dust with the toe of his boot.

"She might have been right, But I am proud you minded her. Don't ride too far."

"I won't. See you." Luke raced for the pinto pony in the pen.

Fleta smiled at the boy's enthusiasm. Then with Noble's strong arm over her shoulder, they went inside the store. Sighing inwardly, she knew she must tell Noble the news before anyone else did. "Rivers sent you a message."

Noble stopped. "Yes?"

"Izer Goodman is in Ft Smith."

"Oh?"

Fleta was puzzled by his flat response. Her blue eyes misted as she looked up in his tired face. He was exhausted, she surmised. "There is something else—Wilbourne Corey came by with a wagon train going to California...he's remarried."

Noble blinked his eyes and then a broad smile crossed his face as he swept her up in his arms. "Well, good, we'll do the same thing."

Fleta laughed as he whirled her around. "Noble, put me down. What will the Osage think?" When he set her on her feet, she spoke softly. "Noble, I don't need a ceremony. I'm already your wife."

Noble shook his head, wondering if he would ever understand women. But it didn't matter. He loved her and would do whatever she wanted to do about getting married. At least it was settled. That swept away most of his tiredness and disgust of the past days.

Before sundown, he went to the stables to check on the gray stallion, feeling guilty for the way he had pushed him. The horse nickered at his approach, but Noble could see that, despite the big horse's strength, he needed several days rest.

"There're new shoes on the bay," Sudan said, from behind him. "I figured you might need a fresh one."

"I'm not looking forward to going either," Noble said his thoughts out loud. Someone had to settle the score with Goodman—other wise the threat of him would never be over.

"I'm going with you," Sudan said softly.

Noble considered the man's words. The Osage could watch the fort in their absence. He knew he could never dissuade the man.

Numb from his days on the move, Noble studied his dusty boot toes. "We'll leave at sunup, we should be there in three days."

"Three days," Sudan echoed softly.

Chapter Eighteen

Fleta lay in bed, staring into the darkness. Noble lay rigid beside her. She knew he was not asleep, yet he seemed distant from her, as though still riding with Custer. Something was bothering him. Maybe the thought of finally facing Izer Goodman. Perhaps something had happened while he was riding with the Seventh Cavalry, something he didn't want to discuss with her.

She raised on her elbow and stared down at him in the dim light from the full moon. "Noble? I know you're not asleep."

"Mmm," he murmured.

"What's wrong?"

"Nothing," he said, but the words came out with an abruptness he hadn't intended.

She tossed back her long braid and peered closely into his face. "What is it?"

"Oh, hell." He gave a great sigh and finally looked at her. "I just wish this whole business with Izer was over."

"Don't go."

"You know I'm going. I couldn't stand the thought of that madman hurting someone else's family."

But she knew that wasn't the only thing on Noble McCurtain's mind. Something deeper than even Izer Goodman was eating at him. Gently she pulled on his arm.

"It won't work...," she murmured, and prevented his reply with a kiss.

Her lips silenced him. If she could not get the truth from him, she knew ways to ease him. With a little coaxing, he moved over her.

In the pink light of pre-dawn, Noble and Sudan prepared to leave. The celluloid collar she had convinced Noble to wear scratched his neck. He promised himself to remove it the moment he was out of sight of the fort. Bad enough she made him wear the new brown suit.

Their goodbyes were solemn. Neither said much.

Noble shook his head as he rode out the gate. They looked like some kind of a circus, him in his new suit and Sudan wearing a fancy beaded doeskin shirt with yard-long fringe. He glanced back at the two pack horses loaded with bedding and food. He saw no sign of either woman in the fort's gateway. He turned back... just as well. Noble ripped off the collar.

The days were hot and sullen. They crossed the Indian Territory swiftly. Just short of Fort Smith, on the road they met and spoke to a Cherokee policeman.

"This man, you ask of, Izer Goodman. He is wanted dead or alive. He must not be in Fort Smith," the tribal lawman said. "But he is very bad man."

"Have you met an Osage by the name of Rivers?" Sudan asked.

"No." The Cherokee shook his head.

"He works for me and sent word that Goodman was there."

"Maybe. It's a big place, but the white man's law is looking for him."

"Thanks," Noble said, anxious to be on their way.

"Well. What do you think now?" Sudan asked as they rode to the ferry.

"Let's find Rivers. Izer may be right under the nose of the law." Noble shook his head ruefully, this time they would locate the outlaw. He would not return home without satisfaction.

As they waited for the ferry on the sandy roadway, Noble decided they would get a hotel room. "Sudan, we'll check in a hotel—"

"That sir, is Arkansas. You get a hotel room and I'll stay with the horses."

Noble frowned at him in puzzlement.

"I know. I been in this land before."

Noble nodded. Sudan had his mind made up, nothing he could say to change it. From beneath his wide brimmed hat, Noble viewed the array of two and three story buildings that made the town look as large as Independence.

They joined two wagons on the ferry for the trip across the Arkansas. Dismounted during the crossing, they each held two of the horses in case they panicked.

"There's a whole street of saloons," Sudan said. "We can look for Rivers there. They have whiskey, women and gambling."

"Be a good place to start," Noble agreed, studying a large bank of afternoon thunderheads forming over the mountains to the north. An eerie foreboding swept him with the cooling winds off the growing storm.

The ferry bumped into the dock. The chugging steam engine forced them to hold the excited horses tighter as the muddy water slapped the sides of the boat.

A train whistle pierced the air, smoke belched from its stack. A paddle boat's shrill whistle added to the bustling city's noise. Even on the rampway, the horses were still excited by all the sights and sounds around them.

Whiskey Row lay ahead. Traffic including drays, wagons, riders on horseback, even some bicycles, surged in all directions. In mid-afternoon, the barkers worked the passersby on the sidewalk, extolling the virtues or sins available at their respective establishments.

Noble rode up behind a parked wagon to speak to one of the men loafing on the sidewalk. "I'm looking for someone," he said, leaning over in the saddle.

"Who?"

"Name's Izer Goodman."

The man looked at the fellow beside him; they both shook their heads blankly. "We don't know him."

"Thanks," Noble said and reined the bay out in the traffic.

He signaled for Sudan to follow with the pack horses.

A woman's loud laughter, followed by a grumble of thunder in the approaching storm, rolled over the sounds in the street.

"Noble!" someone shouted. Both men turned and watched an Indian they barely recognized come across the street, dodging conveyances. Dressed in ragged clothes, Rivers hurried toward them.

"It's Rivers!" Sudan shouted.

Noble nodded, already dismounted. "Are you all right?"

"Plenty good, now you come." The Osage's brown eyes glowed with relief at the sight of his friends.

"Move them damn horses!" a teamster cursed. "This ain't the damn Injun Territory!"

Noble waved Sudan on. He didn't want trouble here. When the freighter passed, Noble gave him a cutting glance before he turned back to Rivers.

"Where is he?"

"Izer is upstairs in a place called Fanny's. He just came back." The Osage pointed to the second story brick building in front of them.

"Is he alone?" Noble asked grimly.

"No. Izer sneaks in to see his woman," River shouted above the wind.

Noble wondered how to get upstairs. A sharp gust swept Noble's hat from his head and thunder rumbled directly over them. He quickly recovered and restored it on his head.

Sudan joined them, obviously he had hitched the horses around the corner for Noble could not see them.

"Are there back stairs?" Noble asked.

"Yes," Rivers said.

"Sudan, you cover the back way out. Rivers, where is he at in the building?"

"Back row, that side," he pointed west. "I have seen him from the roof over there."

Noble studied at the tall brick building; the Osage had been done his job well. "Does he have any of his gang here?"

"No, bunch of breeds stay across the river."

"I can't understand why some law doesn't arrest him."

"Don't know him." Rivers shrugged. "No beard, short hair, no buckskins."

They didn't know the outlaw on sight. Noble nodded in agreement. He didn't have to tell Sudan a thing. The black man and Rivers moved to go around to the alley. Noble's attention was riveted on the second floor. People were hurrying inside as the rain began in earnest. He never noticed the weather as he elbowed his way through the crowd.

Inside the sour smelling, smoke filled barroom, he spied the staircase and started up them.

"Hey, you got business up there?" a bartender challenged him.

Noble swept his coat back exposing his gun holster. "Yes."

The man taken aback, merely nodded. A hush fell over the crowd, the tinkle of glasses faded. Outside the wind and rain rushed around with the roar of a lion. Noble's foot steps caused the stairs to creak in protest.

At the head of the stairs, a young woman, wearing a filmy gauze gown, met him. Her smile faded as she noted the hard look on his face and his right hand on the butt of the Colt. He swept her aside and drew the pistol.

"I want Izer Goodman," he said coldly.

"He ain't here," she lied openly as if to challenge him for rejecting her.

Noble looked down the long hallway to the last side door. "Get downstairs. Now!"

Outside the forces of the storm grew more intense. The gale forces tore at the building. A window shattered below. In one of the rooms, a woman screamed. She stumbled out directly in Noble's path.

"Get out of the way!" he said harshly. She blinked at his gun hand and rushed away.

Other ladies came rushing out of their rooms, frightened by the violent weather battering the building.

"It's going to blow us away," one woman screamed, trying to pull on a duster as she fled by him. "There's a tornado in this!"

Finally Noble stood alone a few steps from the last door on the right. Voices from the room grew louder. Outside, something crashed against the building causing the structure to tremble. Noble tried to imagine the damage, then he drew a deep breath and cocked the hammer back on the .44.

Lifting his foot, he aimed a well placed kick directly at the brass knob, and burst open the door.

Izer Goodman stood on the far side of the bed. His galluses were down, exposing his gray underwear. His cold beady eyes went from Noble to the gun on the dresser. Then he made a try for the weapon.

Noble aimed and fired. Gunsmoke filled the room in a fog, nealy obscuring Izer from his vision. The woman on the bed screamed louder than the storm outside.

Izer made a second attempt to reach the pistol. Slower this time. Blood soaked the left side of his underwear where the first slug found its mark. Noble's next bullet smashed Izer's left eye and the outlaw slipped on the floor.

Noble lowered the smoking gun barrel. It was over. Izer Goodman could not hurt anyone ever again.

Noble backed into the hall and holstered the gun. Still numb, he tried to sort out his thoughts. He opened the back door and faced the full force of rain and wind as he stepped out. Sudan waved to him from the base of the steps.

Noble cast a last glance back at the open door. Yes, Izer was dead. He hurried down the stairs and took the canvas coat from the black man's outstretched arm.

"Izer Goodman will not trouble anyone anymore," Noble said and mounted the bay. "Let's go home." Both men nodded at him. As he rode out of the alley, Noble fought the urge to look back one more time. It was over, he kept reminding himself.

The ferrymen grumbled about the storm, pointing to the rough water in the inky river. Noble felt little patience with the man.

"It's worth a twenty dollar gold piece," Noble said.

"Well, in that case..."

The engine chugged as they left the dock. Noble and his two companions held the horses close as the lights of Fort Smith faded in the abating rain.

Noble knew Fleta was waiting for him. The beautiful woman from Arkansas who became his wife. The cold spray of rain reminded him of their first snow together with the Osage. He closed his eyes—and pictured all them waiting for him in Kansas: Fleta McCurtain, Luke, and the Great Western Company.